His grin was sensual by nature

and mischievous by design. "Have you no enthusiasm for the coming festivities?"

She stifled a grimace. "Festivities," she said. "Is that what you call them? If you want a festive night, you'd do better to invite jugglers and mummers to prance about the chamber."

His black eyes smoldered. "No, my bride. You and I will devise our own entertainment."

The power of speech deserted her. Yet she kept her composure during the toasts and as the people cheered the bride and groom for the last time. Then William rose to his feet.

The dreaded moment had come. In a daze, she stood. Her eyes sought Meg, but the older woman was deep in conversation with Wulfstan and didn't notice.

William guided Emma away from the table and out of the boisterous, oblivious hall. Once they were beyond observation, she pulled her hand from his arm and used her veil as an excuse to occupy her hands elsewhere.

She climbed the spiral, stone stairs as slowly as she dared, delaying the moment when the bedchamber door would close behind them. The stairwell torches were ablaze with flames that eagerly licked the shafts of wood. Behind her, William's footsteps were as loud as thunder.

At the top of the stairs, the large, oak door stood wide open. There was no one inside the bedchamber, not a single soul to grant her one last pardon. Tilda had turned down the bed, and it loomed in the shadows, waiting.

Flight of the Raven

by

Judith Sterling

The Novels of Ravenwood, Book One

Flight of the Raven

Cover Art by *Debbie Taylor*

The Wild Rose Press, Inc.
PO Box 708
Adams Basin, NY 14410-0708
Visit us at www.thewildrosepress.com

Publishing History
First Tea Rose Edition, 2016
Print ISBN 978-1-5092-0946-0
Digital ISBN 978-1-5092-0947-7

The Novels of Ravenwood, Book One
Published in the United States of America

Dedication

This book is dedicated to my parents,
who have always believed in me,
and to my husband,
whose love and support are unconditional.

Chapter One

Northern England, September 1101

"I wonder how eager my bridegroom would be if he knew he could never bed me," remarked Lady Emma of Ravenwood Keep.

Her cousin, Gertrude, exchanged glances with Emma's handmaiden, Tilda, whose normally deft fingers fumbled their attempt to plait Emma's hip-length black hair. An uneasy silence stretched between the three young women, then spiraled out toward the bedchamber walls like a restless spirit.

Gertrude examined her thick braid of chestnut hair, then threw it over her shoulder. "You're making a big mistake," she said.

Emma's violet eyes glowed with resolve. "I'm making the best of an impossible situation."

Gertrude groaned. "The curse. I would expect the cottars and villeins to believe such hogwash, but why do you?"

Emma's gaze fell to the herb-strewn rushes on the floor, and she pressed a hand to her chest. "You know why."

"Your fate is not your mother's. Or your grandmother's, for that matter. Grow up, Emma."

"You wouldn't make so light of the curse if you were in my place."

"Nor would I give my hand in marriage to a thieving, Norman bastard. But as you say, I'm not in your place."

"Done," Tilda said, securing Emma's braid. Then she cleared her throat. "Begging your pardon, but he's not a bastard."

"He might as well be," said Gertrude, her green eyes ablaze. "He's a second son, so he couldn't inherit. But for reasons that pass understanding, he gained Ravenwood."

"The king rewards his best," Emma said. "Sir William is a great warrior."

Gertrude snorted. "Great indeed! He's a ruthless Norman knight, like any other. His supposed valor is doubtless as embroidered as the Ravenwood curse."

Emma's thoughts reeled. *William l'Orage. William the Storm. Could a man who inspires such terror on the battlefield show compassion?*

"You're trembling, my lady," Tilda said. "Shall I stoke the fire?"

Emma attempted a smile, then abandoned the effort. "Only if you are cold," she said, standing. She moved to the window, opened the oak shutters, and peered out at a day that would shape the rest of her life.

Dense fog swirled through the cold morning air. She could scarcely see the bailey below, much less the fertile fields beyond.

"Have you had another vision?" Gertrude asked.

Emma turned her back on the window. "Aye, the same one I've had since my father's death."

"I wondered why you missed supper last night," Gertrude said, "though I should've guessed. When Woden's Circle beckons, you invariably disappear. I cannot understand it."

Tilda's hands found her hips. "'Tis a sacred place."

"'Tis a heathen ring of stones," Gertrude retorted. She turned to Emma. "So you saw the young woman again. Are you certain 'twas your mother? You never knew her."

"I'm positive," said Emma. "She's warning me of danger."

Gertrude frowned. "Yet she says naught and shows you naught."

Emma shrugged. "I cannot force the messages any more than I can control when they come."

"Perhaps she disapproves of your marriage," Gertrude said. "If only you'd been able to wed Aldred. Ravenwood could've stayed a Saxon stronghold, and Aldred would've killed any Norman beast that dared enter our lands."

Emma gave her a pointed look. "That's exactly what I wish to avoid. I've had a bellyful of the hatred between Saxons and Normans. Aldred the Merciless has no place here. My people deserve peace."

Gertrude crossed her arms and stared at Emma. "How do you know Sir William brings peace?"

I don't, Emma thought. *I hope.*

"King Henry wants harmony in the north," she said aloud. "If he trusts Sir William with that task, who are we to doubt? I will do my duty."

Gertrude scowled. "Is it duty or dissent to spurn your husband's right to the marriage bed?"

Emma glanced at the large, oak bed which seemed to swallow a third of the chamber. "I'll be a faithful wife in all other respects," she said. "Better to face a husband's wrath than die in childbirth."

Tilda's brown eyes widened. "Sir William is no ordinary husband. Is it wise to refuse him?"

"Wise or no, my decision is final," Emma said.

She tugged at the long sleeves of her pink, floor-length inner tunic while scrutinizing her gray overtunic's embroidered hem. Though she preferred close-fitting garments, today's attire seemed too tight. Even the air felt close, bound by stone walls which now rang with the slam of the door.

Gertrude was gone. Finally.

Emma paced, filling the bedchamber with the scents of lavender and thyme and the rhythmic crunch of rushes underfoot.

"My head aches," Tilda said.

Emma halted. "A strong dose of woundwort will set it right. Shall I fetch some?"

"Thank you, my lady, but no. 'Twill pass now that we're alone."

Emma sighed. "Gertrude means well."

Tilda pushed a wayward strand of fiery red hair from her face. "Does she? She may be a year older than you, but that doesn't make her smarter. Must she always poke her nose into your affairs?"

"She has nowhere else to poke it. Are you sure you need no medicine?"

"I'm sure."

Emma started to pace anew. "In sooth, I'd prefer the errand to brooding in here, waiting an eternity for Sir William's arrival."

Tilda cleared her throat, and the sound carried a feeling of dread. "My lady?" she said.

Emma paused mid-step and turned to her. "What is it?"

Slowly, Tilda dragged her gaze from the massive bed back to Emma. "When will you tell him?"

Emma swallowed the sudden lump in her throat. "The wedding night."

"Not before?"

"I dare not. What if he refused my hand? The last thing we need is Aldred sniffing at the gate again."

Tilda nodded. "I understand, though I could never be so brave."

Emma slouched. "Is that what I am?" She returned to the window and sighed as the frigid wind brushed her cheeks. The weather had changed little.

Mist. Endless fog. A future hidden.

All at once, she felt the pull, a familiar stirring in the pit of her stomach and in the secret, timeless dimension of her soul. It reached out, yearned to answer the call of Woden's Circle. Another vision awaited her. Maybe this time, its message would be clear.

Emma closed and bolted the shutters, then whirled around. She marched across the chamber and dropped onto a stool.

"What are you doing?" Tilda asked.

"I'm going to the circle." Emma quickly replaced her slippers with low, leather boots.

Tilda stared. "Now?"

"Now."

Emma stood and snatched her gray, woolen mantle from a wooden peg on the wall.

"But you can't," Tilda said, wringing her hands. "What if Sir William arrives while you're gone?"

Emma knelt before a large, intricately carved chest and lifted the lid. She slid her hand past a profusion of soft linen and clasped the cool, hard shape of a key.

"With any luck, he won't."

"And if he does?"

"I'll explain when I return."

"You mean you'll tell him of your visions?"

The heavy lid of the chest plunked closed as Emma stood. "Mayhap I'll lie."

Tilda raised her eyebrows. "He could arrive at any moment. What if he sees you leaving the gatehouse?"

Emma dangled the key from her fingers. "That's what bolt-holes are for."

Tilda's mouth fell open.

"Only you will know I'm gone," said Emma, "and where I've gone. Now, come! We haven't a moment to lose."

Emma threw open the chamber door and descended the long, spiral staircase with the quick, sure-footedness of one who'd memorized each stone step. Her conscience whispered that she was taking an unnecessary risk. Custom and courtesy agreed: Sir William would expect and deserve to be greeted by Ravenwood's mistress. She had no wish to offend him and no idea how he'd react if she did.

But she'd never denied Woden's Circle. Its pull was too strong.

At the bottom of the stairs, Emma grabbed a torch from the wall. She could hear the servants bustling about the great hall, completing last minute preparations for Sir William's arrival. Muttering a quick prayer for invisibility, she slipped past the hall's arched entrance and hurried into the solar. She crossed the room with Tilda close at her heels.

Emma passed the torch to her handmaiden. "Hold this." She dropped to her knees and shoved aside a large rush mat, revealing a trapdoor in the planked floor.

"I don't suppose you'd change your mind?" Tilda asked.

Emma thrust the key into the trapdoor's lock.

"I guess not," Tilda said.

Emma swung the door upward and reclaimed the torch. "Replace the mat," she ordered. "Then put a new torch at the base of the stairs."

Wide-eyed, Tilda nodded. "I'll say a prayer for you, my lady."

"Thank you. I may need it."

Emma descended the narrow, wooden steps to the dark basement below. Once her feet touched ground, she looked up and caught a final glimpse of Tilda's worried face. Then the trapdoor thudded shut.

Well, Emma thought, squaring her shoulders, *that's that.*

She held the torch in front of her, thankful for its heat and light. This small chamber had always seemed a cold, lonely place. Stone more than a yard thick separated it from the rest of the basement. Only the trapdoor above and the secret bolt-hole offered access.

Barrels of spices and chests full of coins, jewels, plate, and cloth crowded the room, but she ignored them. Instead, she moved toward a large tapestry which dominated the opposite wall, ceiling to floor. Heavy and exquisite, its faded threads depicted a wild boar hunt. She pulled the tapestry away from the wall, then slid between fabric and stone until she reached a small, battened door.

She raised the bolt and opened the door. Her torch flickered as a rush of dank, musty air whistled along the narrow passageway beyond. Wrinkling her nose at the smell, she stooped and entered the tunnel. She closed the door behind her and made a mental note to rebolt it later. Then she started toward the small circle of light up ahead.

The tunnel was alive with the squeaks and rustlings of creatures scurrying along the damp stone walls. But while the animals sought shelter from the moaning wind, Emma longed to be a part of it. Outside was freedom, nature's savage dance, and the magic of Woden's Circle.

Finally, she emerged into the thicket. The air was crisp and clean. She plunged the torch into the moist earth and tossed it back into the tunnel. Then she made her way through the tangle of shrubbery which opened onto the vast orchard outside the curtain wall.

Fog still blanketed the land, but it didn't matter. She would've known the way blindfolded. Smiling, she skittered past fruit-heavy trees to the open meadow beyond.

She had made it!

She glided over the grass as though carried on the singing wind. Before, the mist was a barrier. Now it seemed an extension of her body and her innermost self.

A cloak of reverence settled over her shoulders as she climbed and crested the low hill to Woden's Circle. Nine weathered, evenly spaced stones, twice her height, formed a perfect ring. At its center, three larger stones created the appearance of a gateway.

Emma entered the circle and approached the ancient threshold. She stepped in and stretched her arms to touch the slick, cool stones on either side. Then she stilled.

The fog thinned, and she looked to the forest that bordered most of the circle. The Long Wood was a kingdom unto itself with towering sentinels of pine, beech, and the sacred oak. A rustle sounded within. A moment later, a raven emerged. It landed on one of the ring-stones just as two more ravens appeared. Each bird settled onto a different stone.

My little guardians, Emma thought with a smile.

She closed her eyes and inhaled fresh air laced with the scent of pine needles. As she exhaled, the morning's tension coursed downward, out of her body and into the earth. She cleared her mind and slowed her breathing. Each breath brought a deeper peace, a sense of belonging.

At last, her hands tingled with the familiar energy that seemed to flow directly from stone to flesh. Warmth cascaded through her arms and down the length of her body. A primordial power vibrated beneath her feet. The world outside melted away as Woden's Circle wove its magic.

****

Sir William l'Orage rode toward his future like the dark tempest his name implied. Defying custom, he had dressed for battle. Over his chain mail hauberk, he wore a flowing mantle as black as the powerful, aggressive stallion beneath him. Knight and warhorse moved in unison, pushing through the enveloping fog with strength of purpose that brooked no refusal. They had come to conquer.

Beside William rode a second mail-clad knight, his younger brother, Robert. Their squires and William's numerous retainers followed, leading destriers, palfreys, and packhorses laden with weaponry and the tangible wealth of Ravenwood's new lord.

Robert grinned sidewise at his brother. "Always the tactician," he said.

William nodded. "In an enemy land, a strong first impression is crucial."

"Are you certain this is an enemy land?"

"'Tis Saxon."

Robert gestured toward William's savage destrier. "One look at Thunder would impress any rebel, Saxon or Saracen."

Hearing his name, Thunder pricked up his ears. The warhorse reared, lashing out with his great hooves, but William casually curbed the animal.

"As would the ease with which you control him," Robert added.

A sudden gust whipped William's black hair from his face and revealed a fierce smile. "Intimidation is a powerful deterrent."

"One that will serve us well during your nuptials," Robert replied.

William's black eyes narrowed. "We must present a strong, united front, not only to Ravenwood's people, but to a certain honored guest."

"Your new neighbor?"

William clasped the geometrically patterned hilt of his double-edged sword. "Precisely."

"Aldred the Merciless," Robert hissed. "I confess I'd hoped never to meet him. 'Tis a miracle we avoided him in the Holy Land."

"We were too busy storming Jerusalem," William said.

Robert adjusted his mantle, which perfectly

matched his steel gray eyes. "And what of his younger brother?"

"Wulfstan? There are rumors of sorcery. 'Tis even said his moods control the weather."

Robert chuckled. "Do you suppose he's nearby? Fog this thick could mean only one thing."

"That his temper matches his brother's?"

"You read my mind."

"I'd rather read my neighbors'."

Robert sobered. "Or it could mean treachery."

"We may know on the morrow." William shrugged beneath the familiar weight of his mail. "Our guests should reach Ravenwood by noon."

"Your spies are thorough."

William stared hard into the unfathomable mist. *Aye*, he thought. *My scouts have a talent for detail, but there is one question they cannot answer.*

"Lady Emma," he murmured. Her name felt strange on his lips, like the whispering desert winds that stirred the fragrant, exotic spices of the East. *Will you warm my bed without a struggle? Will you give me sons?*

"William?" said Robert.

William blinked and turned to his brother.

"Your silence is deafening," Robert said. "What are your thoughts?"

"That I'll finally have land and a dynasty to inherit it."

"My desires course that same river, but what of love? The bards sing—"

"They sing of tripe!"

Thunder sensed his master's mood and reared again. William asserted his authority, and the stallion instantly obeyed.

"Lady Emma might disagree," Robert said. "She's young enough to believe in romantic verse."

"She's nearly twenty," William responded.

"Then she can hardly object to a bridegroom who's twelve years her senior."

"She has no choice in the matter."

Robert fell silent, but his lips twitched.

A shadow loomed in William's memory. "Come, my bride awaits me." He spurred Thunder into a gallop as though the Devil clawed at his heels.

Not long afterward, he brought Thunder to a trot and peered into the distance. Alongside him, Robert slowed his own warhorse.

"Finally," said Robert, "the fog is lifting."

William's gaze was riveted by a towering shape seemingly condensed from the retreating mist. Perched on a tall hill, Ravenwood Keep rose four floors above its basement storerooms. Each of its four corners boasted a tower, and the walls shone white from a recent application of lime. A high, stone curtain wall surrounded the keep at a distance of forty yards and looked down on a broad, deep moat.

"Impressive," said Robert. "The masons who built it must've been Norman or at least inspired by Norman design."

"And this is only one of Lady Emma's holdings," William said.

Robert grinned. "Soon to be your holdings."

William nodded. The castle looked impregnable, but he'd conduct a thorough inspection anon. Once Ravenwood was secure, he'd see to the other manors.

A sudden movement caught his eye. Atop the

gatehouse, a single raven watched their approach with seeming interest. Its wings fluttered as a harsh, grating sound erupted from the portcullis below.

"'Twould appear we're welcome," Robert said.

The drawbridge lowered, and the brothers rode side by side across it. Countless times in and out of battle, they'd faced the unknown together. Today was no exception.

The clop-clop of hooves on wood punctuated William's every glance. His gaze darted from water to stone, alert to potential threats. Once inside the bailey, he reined in his destrier and searched again for any danger. He found none, only servants pausing in their work to study him. He cataloged their faces one by one. Some held fear; some, curiosity. But there was no hostility, until he looked toward the keep's entrance.

A woman in green emerged from the forebuilding's shadowed archway. She froze at the head of the long, stone staircase that led to the bailey floor and fixed on William a glacial stare.

"Do you suppose that's Lady Emma?" Robert mused.

William frowned. He wasn't certain what he'd expected but surely not the cold brunette barring the entrance.

"Well?" said Robert.

With a sidelong glance, William muttered, "I'm about to find out." He dismounted his warhorse in a quick motion perfected through years of combat. Then he spotted his squire among the throng of retainers. "Geoffrey!"

A brown-haired, strapping lad of sixteen loped forward. "Sir?"

"See to Thunder," William ordered.

"Aye, sir." Geoffrey reached for the stallion's reins.

Swiftly, William turned and strode toward the keep. His fingers grazed the hilt of his sword as the statue on the stairs came to life. Her gaze glued to her feet, she descended to the bailey with slow, measured steps. At last, she lifted her head and met his stare.

"Lady Emma?" he questioned.

The maid's eyes were as green as her tunic. "No," she replied.

When she offered nothing further, he asked, "And you are?"

"Her cousin, Gertrude."

"I see."

Stubborn silence clung to the woman like odor to a cesspool.

His jaw tightened. "Where is Lady Emma?"

"I know not."

"She didn't wish to greet me?"

Gertrude shrugged.

Heat pricked his skin. "Where did you last see her?"

"In her bedchamber."

"And she said naught of her plans?"

Gertrude scowled. "She doesn't always consult me."

At that moment, a short, plump maidservant raced down the stairs. Her brown eyes were huge as they scanned him from head to toe. She dropped a quick curtsy, then whispered in Gertrude's ear.

William clenched his fists. "Who is this?"

Gertrude's eyes were now as wide as the servant's.

"Tilda," she said. "Emma's handmaiden."

Tilda curtsied again. "Sir," she offered in a shaky voice.

"What are you about, girl?" William asked.

Tilda and Gertrude shared a nervous glance.

"Speak up," William ordered. "Have you news of your mistress?"

The handmaiden gulped. "She's gone, sir."

William stiffened. "What?"

Tilda's face flushed, and she wrung her hands. "Not gone forever. Just for a time."

"Where?" William snapped.

"Half a mile in that direction," Gertrude said, pointing, "at the top of the hill near the Long Wood. Look for the stone circle."

William nodded curtly, then spun on his heel. He stalked the short distance to his men.

"Geoffrey!" he bellowed. "My horse!"

The squire jumped aside as William vaulted into the saddle. Thunder reared, excited by the emotion surging through his master. William checked the stallion's movements, willing Thunder in the direction of the gatehouse.

"William!" Robert shouted above the clamor of soldiers, horses, and castle servants who now hurried back to work.

William turned to him. "It seems my bride is reluctant after all."

"Was that gorgon in green your—"

"No," said William, "though I begin to doubt whether Lady Emma will prove any sweeter."

"So where is she?"

"A half-mile hence."

Robert frowned. "Insupportable!"

"Indeed," said William, his heels poised to spur Thunder to action. "But willing or no, my bride shall learn some manners!"

Chapter Two

Emma's vision unfurled. At first, she saw only mist. Its hue grew darker, richer, suffused with violet. Floating dreamlike, she backed away. The farther the distance, the clearer the shape. The violet mist became the iris of an eye; the eyes graced the face of a woman remembered not from life, but from vision. 'Twas her mother, Margaret, whose expression bespoke her fear more eloquently than words.

The vision had always ended at this point, but now it continued. Emma drifted farther away from the image to glimpse her mother's entire frame. Margaret's delicate hands caressed her swollen belly; she was pregnant.

Is this your warning, Mother? To remind me of the danger of childbirth?

Margaret remained silent.

Please, speak to me.

Slowly, Margaret lifted a hand from her stomach and stretched out her arm. She pointed to something behind Emma.

This is it, Emma thought as her dream-self began to turn.

The sudden rumble of horse hooves yanked her from the trance. She blinked and gulped a breath of cool, damp air. Then she dropped her hands from the stones on either side.

I was so close, she thought, shaking her head.

"Lady Emma?" a deep, male voice snapped from behind.

She spun around.

At the edge of Woden's Circle loomed a figure dark as midnight's soul. The wind whipped the man's sable, jaw-length hair into a frenzy about the smooth, hard lines of his clean-shaven face. His thick, black mantle was a living thing, swirling around his tall, imposing frame as though it fought to contain the raw masculinity within.

Emma steeled herself. "Who wishes to know?" she asked, though her words were more bravado than question. He could be only one man.

"Sir William l'Orage," he said in a low, controlled voice.

She shivered, then willed her body to cease its foolish reaction. "I am she."

William stood perfectly still for several long, excruciating seconds.

She'd intended to approach him, but her feet remained rooted to the ground. She just stood there, returning his stare with equal intensity.

He's studying me, she thought, *as if I were some citadel to which he might lay siege.*

Suddenly, he advanced toward her. Each step was powerful, potent. The closer he came, the stronger was his presence.

He halted an arm's length away, and she fancied his aura reached out to hers. His energy was virile, brimming with authority, and in a strange new way, attractive.

"Did you forget my arrival today?" His voice was

calm, but his clear, black eyes glistened with a darker emotion.

She tore her gaze from his, then returned it an instant later. "I didn't forget. I merely lost track of time."

"'Twas your duty to greet me, and you *shall* greet our guests in future."

She bristled. "I know my duty. You need not fear on that count."

"Nor any count," he said. "I fear nothing."

Without warning, the shadow of the Ravenwood curse eclipsed her irritation, transforming an angry comeback into a wistful sigh. "How nice for you," she said. "I would I shared that talent."

William seemed to consider her words. Then his black eyes thawed. "'Tis more experience than talent."

Emma wondered what he'd endured to chase away even the demons of hell. "I should've been there to greet you," she said at last. "Forgive me."

His brow smoothed. "Of course."

She performed a tentative smile. "You found me in my favorite place."

"Thanks to your cousin."

"But how did she—"

"Your handmaiden."

"Tilda." Emma nodded. "I imagine the situation was awkward."

The picture of nonchalance, William folded his arms. "Quite."

A loud croak sliced the air amid a flutter of wings.

Emma grinned. "*Hremmas*," she said.

William cocked an eyebrow. "What?"

"Ravens." She gestured to the party of birds that

shifted from stone to stone. "'Tis the Saxon word."

He nodded. Then he turned his head and stared into the shadowed forest.

"You'll find them always underfoot," she said.

"Hence the name of the estate." He turned back to her.

"Aye, so I hope you like them."

"As well as any creature."

Emma could think of nothing to say.

William contemplated her for another long moment, then unfolded his arms. His hand skimmed the hilt of his sword.

"Come," he said. "Let's return to the keep."

She hesitated, then stepped out of the stone doorway which had seemed a haven. A blast of cold air grabbed her cloak, and she felt even more vulnerable. The wind was now sharp and demanding.

Pulling her mantle close about her, she walked beside her future husband. She accepted his silence and kept a comfortable distance between them.

Outside the sacred circle, she paused. A black beast regarded her with giant eyes.

"What's his name?" she asked.

"Thunder," William answered.

The warhorse neighed fiercely at the sound of his name.

"It suits him," Emma said, then in a wry tone added, "as he suits you."

William stopped abruptly, but she continued on toward the animal.

"Good day to you, Thunder," she cooed. She touched his side experimentally.

The stallion's muscles twitched beneath her hand.

He seemed to exude a power equal to his master's. Yet Thunder calmed and whinnied when she lengthened the caress. Her fingers traced a slow pattern over the animal's smooth, shiny coat, and she lost herself in the pleasure of the moment.

Like a clever thief, William appeared at her side. She looked up, startled. Eyes the color of Satan's dreams bore into hers, sending a rush of alarm to the base of her spine.

"Most people fear him," William murmured.

Emma lifted her chin. "I am not most people."

"Evidently."

William's large hands slid beneath her woolen mantle and locked around her waist. She was about to protest when he hoisted her onto Thunder's back. Then he swung himself into the saddle behind her.

She avoided his gaze. He was too close, too warm.

"I prefer to walk," she said.

"Nonsense." He prompted Thunder with his knightly spurs. The warhorse began to move.

She frowned. "Do you make a habit of denying ladies' requests?"

"Not as a rule."

"I see," she said, but she didn't. Nor did she care at the moment.

Her bridegroom was a stranger and an arrogant one at that. She would hold her tongue. He might think her rude, but her well of conversation had run dry. For the short ride home, she focused on the expansive countryside, where hill and dale lay abandoned by the morning mist.

****

'Twas the first moment he'd had to himself in over

a sennight. William relaxed into a high-backed, oak chair and familiarized himself with his new surroundings. The lord's solar was a warm space, brightened by a roaring fire and colorful tapestries. He would enjoy it in the years to come, as he would enjoy his wife.

Lady Emma.

His blood stirred at the thought of her. She had seemed a vision, a raven-haired temptress standing as proud and erect as the pagan stones that flanked her. Her violet eyes sparkled with intelligence and warmth, even after he'd provoked her ire. And when she laid her dainty hand on Thunder's flesh...

William shuddered. How would it feel to be touched so? By her hand, by candlelight? Her caress would shame the pleasures of Heaven and ease the torments of Hell.

With a sudden grumble, he shifted in his chair. Was he a pip-squeak boy to harden at the mere thought of a maid? To imagine she possessed some angelic quality which could help him forget? No. 'Twas folly, madness. To bare one's soul to a woman was to have it trod upon.

At that moment, Robert breezed into the solar. "You look like the very Devil," he said with a grin.

William regarded his brother's dimpled smile in stony silence.

"Come now," Robert prodded. "Leave off your black thoughts and admit you're pleased. Your bride is as comely a maid as ever I've seen."

"She is that."

"And she seemed suitably demure when you brought her back."

"Demure, though apparently unwell."

Robert raised a questioning eyebrow.

"Upon our return, the lady pleaded illness and retired to her chamber," William explained.

"She looked well enough from where I stood."

"Quite."

"I suppose one can hardly blame her."

William crossed his arms and stared at his brother.

"Really," Robert continued, "between your fiery temper and that black monster of a horse, 'tis a wonder she didn't sprint to the top of the highest tower."

William's gaze slid to the fire which crackled and hissed in the grate. "She had no fear of Thunder."

"Ah," said Robert, "then you're the monster."

William ripped his stare from the flames and leveled it at his brother. But a smile tugged at his lips. "Your support overwhelms me."

"As well it should," said Robert. He crossed the room, claimed the chair next to William, and stretched out his legs. "This is a comfortable solar."

William nodded. "Equal to our brother's, I dare say."

"Hugh may have inherited Seacrest, but he must still get a wife. You're ahead of us both on that score."

William returned his attention to the massive fireplace.

Robert cleared his throat. "While you were fetching your runaway bride, I picked up some new information."

"About?"

"Lady Emma."

William looked up from the fire. "Well?"

"There's a ridiculous rumor circulating the keep

about a curse," Robert declared.

Amusement tickled William's lips. "Oh?"

"Aye," said Robert. "For two hundred years, every Lady Ravenwood has died in the attempt to bear an heir."

"Indeed?"

"Invariably."

"What more do the people say?"

"More?"

"Fairy-tale curses usually have a cure, do they not?"

Robert unleashed a broad smile. With dramatic flair, he pointed at William. "Right," he said. "The only remedy is true love."

William snorted. "A rare commodity."

"Nonexistent, to hear you tell it," Robert quipped. "But if a Ravenwood heir were conceived in love, the curse would end."

William fell silent. He knew firsthand the pitfalls of love, true or otherwise.

"I wonder," said Robert, "does Lady Emma share the people's belief?"

"Certainly not."

"'Tis possible, though."

"And as probable as seating a king below the salt."

Robert shrugged, then turned away as a horn sounded from the great hall. Seconds later, Geoffrey and Robert's towheaded squire, Guy, appeared in the doorway.

"Dinner, sir," Geoffrey announced.

William nodded and stood.

Robert followed suit. "I still say gossip may have colored Lady Emma's opinion," he said. "These Saxons are a superstitious lot."

"Perhaps," William replied, starting toward the door, "but make no mistake. By Midsummer next, I shall have an heir."

Chapter Three

The next morning, Emma basked in the myriad scents of her garden. The sun stared down at her through a sky as blue as the bundle of cornflowers in her hand. The flower petals had many uses. They colored ink and garnished vegetable dishes, and Emma herself used them to heal the various wounds and digestive disorders of the keep's inhabitants.

If only there were some magical medicine to rid me of duty, she thought.

Her feigned illness the day before had allowed her to take both dinner and supper alone in her chamber. She had needed air, a chance to think. On swift wings, morning had come, but it brought no answers.

So she'd come to her garden to lose herself in clipping weeds and collecting herbs. She crouched over her work with enthusiasm, absorbing the resilience of the moist, rich soil. The natural rhythm of daily tasks was like a balm. Even the clangs from the smithy and the clucking of hens comforted her.

A shadow fell over her, and she started.

"Gracious," a familiar voice said behind her.

Emma heaved a sigh as she stood and turned. 'Twas just Meg.

Old Meg was the only mother figure Emma had ever known. No one knew her age, but she was the twin sister of Emma's great-grandmother and her mother's namesake. She was also the one living person with eyes the exact shade of Emma's. Alert and spry, the elderly woman had taught Emma all she knew about plants, healing, and friendship.

The sunlight danced in Meg's eyes. "I didn't mean to frighten you, child."

Emma shrugged and expelled a nervous giggle. "No matter. Even a pigeon might scare me this morning."

"Is he so terrifying?"

"My bridegroom?"

"Who else?"

Emma looked down at her handful of flowers, noting for the first time that their color matched her attire. As she stared, one blue seemed to bleed into the other.

"Emma?" Meg prompted.

Bright violet eyes met an older, almost identical pair. "'Tis difficult to explain."

Meg crossed her arms, causing the loose, gray folds of her tunic to shift like a storm cloud gliding through a restless sky. "Try," she said gently.

Emma took a deep breath. "He...bothers me."

"Interesting."

"Annoying, I'd say."

"Was he unkind to you?"

Emma kicked a wayward pebble. "He had the gall to lecture me on duty."

"Had he need to?"

"Hardly." Emma stooped to pick up her basket of collected plants. "I eat, drink, and sleep duty."

Meg stepped closer and peered into Emma's basket. "Dittany. Are Father Cedric's joints paining him again?"

"Unfortunately."

"And horehound. Has someone a cough?"

"No, but winter will arrive soon enough."

"'Tis wise to prepare for the future, however uncertain it may be."

Meg's words encompassed more than weather or medicine, and Emma knew it. With a sigh, she dropped the cornflowers into her basket. "If only there were no curse."

"I know, child." Meg took the basket. "If I could lift that burden, I would in a heartbeat."

Emma searched Meg's eyes. Anguish glistened within them.

"You were lucky," Emma said. "You escaped wedlock."

Meg nodded. "My sister married instead."

Emma trembled despite the sun's warmth. "And then she died in childbirth."

Meg stood motionless. "I want to ask you something. If the curse were lifted, how would you feel about Sir William?"

Emma frowned. "What are you asking?"

"Are you attracted to him?"

A sly memory crept into Emma's mind. Black, abysmal eyes pierced hers. Fierce masculinity—too near, and yet not near enough—prickled her skin.

"You're blushing," Meg remarked.

Emma's hands flew to her cheeks. They were hot, mutinous.

Meg grinned. "I thought as much."

"What?"

"You're a smart girl. I trow you understand."

Emma pursed her lips. "I'm glad I amuse you."

"And I'm glad an attraction exists."

"Yet if I heed it, I could die."

Meg sobered. "I see your point. Forgive me."

"There's naught to forgive," Emma said. "Walk with me."

Together, they navigated the garden paths and started toward Emma's workshop.

"I only wish things were different," Emma said.

Meg laid a hand on Emma's back. "Perhaps they will be, if you give them time."

"Time is not a luxury I possess."

Just then, they encountered two young laundresses hanging sheets and tablecloths in the courtyard.

"Good morrow, Ethel, Winifred." Emma nodded to each in turn.

The servants looked up from their work. "Good morrow, my lady."

"Is your supply of wood ash holding out?" Emma inquired.

"Aye, my lady." Ethel adjusted her headrail.

"Good." Emma continued on with Meg.

A few steps farther, a slim, ungainly boy of ten scampered toward them with broom in hand.

"How fares your puppy, Edwin?" Emma asked.

"Very well, my lady," the stableboy said, "since you mended his leg."

"And your mother," said Emma, "is she using the poultice I gave her?"

Edwin nodded. "Every day, and she's much the better for it. But she'll be needing more soon."

"I'll see to it," Emma promised.

"Thank you, my lady," Edwin said.

Emma smiled fondly at him as he scurried off to the stable.

"You've such an eye for detail," Meg murmured. "I'm amazed you haven't noticed."

Emma stopped at the entrance to her workshop. "Have I overlooked something?"

Meg lowered her eyes. "Nothing of consequence. Come, let's get to work."

As the older woman disappeared through the doorway, Emma paused to consider her cryptic remark. But, finding no solution, she shook it off and followed Meg inside.

****

"I'll expect a ready supply of weapons, bowstrings, and arrows," William ordered, his towering, muscular frame blocking the armory's only exit. His inspection was complete.

"Aye, sir," said the castle's stout and painfully nervous armorer. The man's blue eyes seemed to bulge from their sockets.

"My men brought their own weaponry, but they'll need more if there's a siege," William continued. "And I'll not have the locals ill-equipped for their service. All weapons must be kept in prime condition."

"Always, sir," the armorer pledged.

William nodded his approval. "I'll hold you to it," he said in a clear, resonant tone which carried to all servants in the vicinity.

Satisfied, he withdrew and started across the bailey. Ravenwood buzzed with activity. The grooms in the stable fed the horses and swept the stalls. The smith pounded out horseshoes at his forge, while close by, knights and their squires plunged and parried in swordplay. Scullions carried buckets of water from the well to the kitchens, from whence streamed the tantalizing smell of roasting meat.

William drank in the scent, and his stomach rumbled. He was about to explore the kitchens when he spotted Tilda scuttling toward the keep.

"Tilda!" he shouted above the din.

The handmaiden froze as he closed the distance between them.

"Sir William," she answered, clasping her hands together.

"Where is your mistress?" he asked.

Tilda swallowed hard. "She was headed for her workshop when last I saw her."

"Workshop?"

She pointed over her shoulder. "The wooden hut near the herb garden. She should still be there."

"Good," said William. "Go about your work."

Tilda curtsied, then hurried away.

His steps quickened as he approached the hut, but once there, he lingered beside the entrance. Emma and a veiled woman stood with their backs to the door. Absorbed in their work, they huddled over a large, wooden table.

He noted at once the neatness of the space. His bride obviously respected discipline and order, at least in her workshop. Flagons, jars, and stoppered bottles of all sizes lined the long, well-dusted shelves. Equidistant bunches of dried herbs hung in straight rows from the wooden beams above.

Amid the familiar scents of plants like basil and cowslip, an alien, pungent odor tickled his nostrils. He fought and defeated a sneeze, but the women sensed his presence all the same. They turned together, and two extraordinary pairs of eyes met his stare.

"Sir William," Emma said.

"My lady." With a casual air, he stepped over the threshold.

Emma motioned to the older woman. "This is Meg."

He nodded to Meg. Her eyes lit up, and she flashed him a miraculously even-toothed smile. The action created a grid of wrinkles from her mouth to the corners of her eyes.

She turned to Emma. "Shall I stay or go?"

"Leave us," William said.

"Of course," Meg responded. Still beaming, she slipped from the hut.

He returned his attention to Emma. Their gazes locked, and for several seconds, neither one moved.

Abruptly, she straightened and lifted her chin. "Was it necessary to dismiss her?"

You're a bold one, he thought with a smile. Why it pleased him, he couldn't say.

He stepped closer to her. "She was more than willing to go."

Emma leaned back against her worktable. "Why are you here?"

"Why not?"

"A direct answer will suffice."

His mouth twitched. "I wanted to inquire after your health."

She lowered her eyes. "Oh. I feel better today."

"I'm glad to hear it."

Her bewitching, violet eyes looked up at him. His stomach dropped.

Easy now, he cautioned himself.

"I'll want you by my side to greet our guests," he said aloud.

"Aldred and Wulfstan," she said.

William nodded. "What do you know of them?"

"I know Aldred isn't half the man his brother is," Emma said hotly.

He frowned. "Explain."

"Aldred preens himself over his military prowess and the fear he inspires in Nihtscua's people."

"Nihtscua Keep. His estate to the north."

"Aye. He has no honor, only an insatiable lust for blood."

"And power?"

"By the barrelful."

"What can you tell me of Wulfstan?"

"He's as different from Aldred as water from stone. His only hunger is for knowledge."

"Of what?"

"The workings of our world and the realms beyond."

"Magic?"

"Some call it that."

"I see. A man of mystery."

"He is that," Emma said in a softer voice, "but he has a quiet dignity, too. Those who fear Wulfstan misjudge his studies and his abilities. In truth, Nihtscua would fare much better were he its master."

William's nostrils flared. Her affection for the Saxon was obvious. It stirred in him a demon which had remained long dormant, but he stifled the emotion as quickly as it had surfaced.

"Nihtscua," he said, in control once more. "What

does it mean?"

"Shadow of night."

"Suitably dark."

She cocked her head to the side. "You think so? 'William the Storm' is hardly a beacon of hope."

He bristled. "You dare flout my name?"

"On the contrary, I admire it. I'll take a good storm over insipid sunshine any day. The writhing clouds and biting wind are far more exciting."

Her words held passion and promise. They sparked an immediate response in him. His manhood was rigid, ready.

For a long moment, she stared into his eyes. Then she cleared her throat and whirled to face her worktable. His gaze burned a trail of desire down her back, following her two long braids to the provocative curves where they stopped.

God's teeth, he cursed inwardly. *How shall I wait until tomorrow night?*

Battling his instincts, he claimed a space beside her at the table's edge. He watched intently as she placed a handful of leaves in a mortar.

"So this is your work," he said.

"Aye." Her gaze fixed on the task. "The people depend on me, and I'm happy to serve."

She wrapped her delicate fingers around a thick, stone pestle. The action did nothing to ease his condition. He had to make conversation, or he'd have his bride on the table faster than a Turk wielded a scimitar.

He pointed to the small pile of red berries beside a cluster of twigs. "What are those?"

"Hawthorn branches and their fruit. You've

probably tasted the berries in jellies and sauces, but a powder made from the seeds is good for the heart. Don't expect to see the blossoms in any of the local cottages, though. 'Tis bad luck, I'm told."

Her wide grin proved she didn't share the belief. He couldn't help grinning back.

"I didn't recognize the plant," he said, "but I've heard the legends. The ancient Greeks and Romans thought it protected them from evil spirits."

"Ah, so you listen to legends too. I thought you only made them."

William didn't know whether to laugh or take offense, but at least his blood had cooled. His gaze dropped to the leaves Emma bruised in the mortar. "What's that there?"

"Mandrake. It can be deadly, but in moderation, it makes a soothing ointment. 'Tis likewise a stimulant."

"How so?" He pretended ignorance. This plant had inspired its own tales.

"It encourages the act of—" She broke off and looked at him. Her amethyst eyes were large, hypnotic.

A new shaft of desire sliced through him. "What does it encourage?"

She opened her mouth, but no sound escaped.

He lowered his gaze to her full, sensual lips. Their natural shade was a deep pink. Almost purple. The upper lip was unusually plump, as ripe and tempting as its counterpart.

In a hushed voice, he continued, "You were saying…"

"I was?"

"You were. Mandrake encourages…"

"Passion."

He inched toward her. He would kiss her, teach her the meaning of the word.

"Oh!" another female cried.

Emma sprang away from him, and his attention snapped to the intruder. Gertrude darkened the doorway.

The chit's green eyes narrowed. "Forgive me."

"State your purpose," he ordered.

Gertrude's gaze shot to Emma. "John would speak with you."

"John is our steward," Emma explained.

"I know," said William. "I met him yesterday, while you dined alone in your chamber."

Color flooded Emma's cheeks. "Oh," she said. "I wasn't informed."

"John awaits you in the kitchen," Gertrude pressed. "He has questions touching the wedding banquet."

Emma started forward, but her foot froze midair. She cast William a sidelong glance. "By your leave," she said.

He nodded. "Proceed."

Her hips swayed as she stepped over the doorsill and disappeared in a flurry of blue. He licked his lips and smiled.

His bride might concern herself with the nuptial feast, but his appetite craved something far more delectable. 'Twould be a wedding night to remember.

Chapter Four

Emma followed her cousin into the sweltering heat of the kitchens, and a heady mixture of spices, roasting meats, and freshly baked bread seduced her senses. The main kitchen was enormous, and its walls rang with the head cook's constant commands. Undercooks lined the trestle tables and hastened to obey. They chopped vegetables, plucked poultry, and pressed pastry dough into huge pie dishes. Some tended the iron cauldrons which hung by hook and chain over the blazing hearth, while others basted a wild boar carcass rotated by the turnspit.

Most were so engrossed in their work that they never noticed the two young women. Sidestepping a trio of hungry, hopeful kittens, Gertrude led Emma to a corner which seemed the only space not in use.

"Where's John?" Emma asked through the clamor.

Gertrude averted her gaze to her yellow tunic. "I've no idea. I lied to save you."

"I needed saving," said Emma.

"The filthy Norman dog," Gertrude spat. "How could you bear to stand so close to him?"

"Oh, I can bear it. The trouble is convincing myself otherwise."

"You cannot be serious."

Emma studied her cousin's face for a long moment. 'Twas difficult to read. "I thought you wanted me to yield to his attentions."

"If you must marry him, aye. But is there no other solution?"

"If by solution you mean Aldred, forget it."

"Why?"

Emma rolled her eyes. "What has that animal ever done to secure your high opinion of him?"

"He's Saxon."

"That doesn't make him good."

"Perhaps not, but if you married him, Ravenwood's blood would remain pure and untainted by Norman swill."

"Really, Gertrude! Has logic so escaped you?"

"You rebuke me? What has logic to do with visions and curses?"

"Some experiences surpass rational thought."

Gertrude looked deflated. "You surely have a gift for attracting them."

Emma watched as a servant pulled a loaf of bread out of the hive-shaped oven in the side of the hearth. A surge of desperate humor sparked a ridiculous thought. *If only childbirth were that easy.*

Priests held definite views on why that wasn't the case, but she secretly rejected them. The God to whom she prayed was benevolent and wise. The heart of love. He wouldn't purposely inflict pain on others.

Gertrude stepped closer. "You must've considered that what you deny Sir William he could take by force."

Emma's chest tightened. "Let's walk to the mews," she said. "This heat is too intense."

After the kitchens, the bailey was heaven. A cool breeze swept through the courtyard like an angel of mercy. It calmed Emma, and she fell into an easy gait beside Gertrude.

As they neared the mews, Gertrude tugged at Emma's sleeve. "You've not replied to what I said inside."

"I'd rather not think about it," Emma said.

"Ignoring the problem won't make it go away."

"I know that."

"Then you'd better consider your options."

They stopped beside the lengthy wooden shed that housed the castle's falcons. The soft tinkle of bells drifted toward them as a hooded, long-winged hawk tested the leather jesses which bound her leg to a weathering block.

At least you're outside, little one, Emma thought. *Be patient. Soon you'll hunt and soar with the best of them.*

"Listen to me," said Gertrude.

Emma pulled her attention from the restless falcon and regarded her cousin.

Mischief glittered in Gertrude's eyes. "Given a choice between Aldred and Sir William, you prefer the latter."

"Without a doubt."

"What if there were a third option?"

"There is none."

"But if there were?"

"I'd strongly consider it."

Gertrude's smile was triumphant, and its brilliance was a reminder of how seldom it appeared. "Then consider Wulfstan."

"Do you know something I don't?"

"No, but hear me out. We know he has no desire to marry."

"Aye. He'd rather be left alone to study and learn in peace. And he doesn't need heirs as Aldred does."

"And if he needs no heirs..."

"He wouldn't require me in his bed."

"Precisely."

"Even so, would Wulfstan agree to such a union?"

Gertrude's fists locked onto her hips. "He's always cared about you. Why would he object? The two of you could run away before the wedding."

"'Twould have to be tonight."

"Aye," Gertrude enthused. She clapped her hands together, and a peregrine inside the mews answered with a high, sharp cry.

"Come," Emma said, starting toward the dovecote. "We're disturbing the falcons."

As they strolled along, she flirted with the new possibility. *To marry a friend. To live without the one responsibility I've dreaded my whole life. To fear nothing, as Sir William claims to do.*

Sir William. She was promised to him, and he wasn't a man to be gainsaid. If by some miracle he released her from the obligation, she'd still be acting against the king's wishes. Only yesterday, she'd stood inside Woden's Circle and insisted that she understood duty. Sir William had seemed to believe her. She couldn't betray his trust.

She halted in front of the dovecote and contemplated the inscrutable pattern of vines clinging to its round, rock walls. Then she closed her eyes to absorb the mellow, flowing calls from the birds within.

"I cannot do it," she said at last.

Gertrude's face crumpled into a mask of disapproval. "Why ever not?"

"Sir William is a man of honor."

"You owe him no loyalty."

"I gave my word."

"Will you give him your maidenhead? He will demand it, and you know he can take it."

Emma stiffened. "He can try."

Gertrude stepped backward. "Well," she said, "I, for one, would like to see that battle."

****

High on the crenellated battlement, William paused to admire the keep's commanding view of the countryside. Beyond the hum of the bailey, sheep grazed on the castle banks, and a patchwork of manor lands stretched far and wide. The fallow fields lay quiet, but others teemed with villeins whisking their scythes through golden shoots of barley. The sight reminded him of the malty smell of newly brewed ale, and the harmony possible between a land and its people during peacetime. 'Twas good to see a harvest of crops instead of human lives.

Malignant memories slithered through his mind, but he axed them and focused on a flurry of movement below. The huntsman, accompanied by his assistants and hounds, plodded across the drawbridge. No doubt the party headed for what the locals called the Long Wood. A part of William longed to join them, to lose himself in the thrill of the chase.

"Ah," a deep voice crooned.

William started. His brother stood beside the stairwell, not ten feet away.

"How long have you been there?" William asked.

Robert sauntered over and joined him along the parapet. "Long enough to know you were brooding again. On the morrow, you shall have a beautiful wife and more land than many barons. Yet you look as though you've been commanded to take up gong farming."

"If I had, I'd insist that you join me."

"I needn't shovel shit to nose it."

"No? What could possibly be ranker?"

"Your moods."

William threw him a caustic look. "You should be a court jester."

"And squander my humor on those who would appreciate it? Never."

William grinned. "The sword does suit you better than the rattle."

"I should hope so. It saved your arse more than once, not to mention mine."

"I'd rather not discuss your arse."

Robert bowed dramatically. Then he straightened and cocked his head toward the hunting party. "What I wouldn't give for a rousing hunt. It seems ages since our last one, and a world away."

"Aye," said William, "but we've no time for that now, not with the impending arrival of our guests."

"The men know your instructions. They'll be armed and watchful, and resplendent in their gear. The squires must've spent half the night polishing blades and mail."

"Good. Aldred will be on the lookout for any sign of weakness."

"Have you questioned Lady Emma about him?"

A pair of sparkling violet eyes invaded William's thoughts. "This morning."

"And?"

William peered into the distance, but he could feel Robert's keen gaze on him. "Our discussion was most illuminating."

After a brief hesitation, Robert said, "Would it kill you to elaborate?"

William grumbled. "Her opinion of Aldred is as foul as ours."

"And Wulfstan?"

William's jaw tightened. "I'm told he's a paragon of virtue."

"Then the lady holds him in high regard."

"If he were any higher, his privy would endanger the angels."

Robert laughed. "I see." He clapped a hand on William's shoulder. "If I didn't know better, I'd say you were jealous."

"Of what? A lisping, deluded wizard?"

"He lisps?"

"He will, minus a few teeth."

"Ha! Mayhap *you* should be a jester."

"Not likely."

The stairwell came to life with the clunk of leather boots stamping on stone. Seconds later, Geoffrey appeared. His cheeks were flushed, and sweat glistened on his forehead.

The squire gulped a lungful of air. "Sir," he breathed, rushing forward. "I had to find you...to tell you. I cannot believe what I just heard!"

"Calm yourself and speak plainly," William instructed.

Geoffrey nodded. "As you requested, I checked on your new peregrine. While I was in the mews, I heard two women outside. One of them was Lady Emma."

The squire hesitated. His wide, amber eyes looked from one knight to the other.

William felt a sting of warning in his gut. "Go on."

"They were talking about the wedding," Geoffrey said. "Lady Emma doesn't want it. She's plotting against you, sir. She wants to marry Wulfstan and run away tonight!"

William's peripheral vision faded. Molten rage tested the limits of his control, but he contained it.

Robert swore under his breath. "William, what will you do?"

In a voice as smooth as a dagger's edge, William said, "I will speak with my wife."

Geoffrey shifted his feet. "Shall I fetch her?"

"No," said Robert. "Allow me."

William regarded his squire. "Return to your work, and tell no one what you heard."

"Understood," said Geoffrey. He hurried down the stairs.

William turned to his brother. "Find her and bring her to the prison tower."

"What?" said Robert.

"'Tis empty, is it not?"

"Aye, but—"

"Do it. I'll be waiting there."

"Your anger is just, but the prison tower?"

William gritted his teeth. "She would dishonor me and defy the king," he said. "If she wants to act like a traitor, let's treat her like one."

Chapter Five

Finally alone, Emma wandered up and down the vegetable garden's neat, straight rows. She felt more like herself than she had all day. She'd made the right decision. Honor and duty were sacred.

So was honesty. There she had faltered.

Her experience with Sir William was limited. Yet his words, behavior, and reputation all attested to his integrity.

And I would make a mockery of it, she thought. *I would stand before our guests, Father Cedric, and the holy cross...and lie.*

She couldn't do it. Despite the risk, she would tell Sir William of her intentions before the ceremony. He deserved that much. Then he could stay or go, and she could face her future with a clear conscience and her virginity intact.

She turned toward the keep, and her stomach dropped. Ten yards away and gaining fast was Sir Robert. His expression looked as black as the hair that framed it. His steel-gray stare was hard and unwavering.

He stopped in front of her. "My lady," he said tightly. "My brother would speak with you."

She endeavored to smile, but his demeanor thwarted her. "Of course," she replied. "Please take me to him."

Not a word was spoken as he briskly led her through the courtyard, into the keep, and toward the tower farthest from Ravenwood's entrance. But when he started up the tower stairway, she hesitated.

"Why are we here?" she asked. "Is Sir William inspecting the prison quarters?"

"No doubt," Robert said without a glance in her direction.

"Aren't they satisfactory?"

"You'll have to ask him."

More perplexed by the minute, Emma followed him up the spiral stairs. When they reached the top, he ushered her into the small, unfurnished chamber. It seemed a hollow shell after the busy, bright expanse of the bailey.

William stood before the cold hearth with his back to the door. His commanding presence diminished the sweeping arch of the vacant fireplace.

"Leave us," he ordered without turning. "Shut the door behind you."

The heavy, oak door slammed shut. The stone walls reverberated from the force of it.

Emma studied the sheen of William's straight, black hair, the proud set of his shoulders, and the wide, leather belt which cinched his ebony tunic at the waist. An eternity might've passed while she waited for him to acknowledge her presence. When at last he turned, his dark eyes blazed.

Her stomach lurched. "Y-you wished to see me?"

He glowered at her in silence. A chill of foreboding ran through her, but she stood her ground.

A full minute later, he still hadn't spoken. Her patience waned. If he expected her to read his mind, he could think again.

She cleared her throat. "You obviously need time to collect your thoughts, so I'll leave you to them."

"You will stay right here," he ruled in slow, measured words. His scorching gaze belied his smooth tone of voice. "I sent for you to discuss your betrayal."

She swore under her breath. Someone must've divulged her plan to stay celibate. If only she'd told him sooner.

"I can explain," she said.

"Save your breath. There's only one explanation."

"You said 'discuss.' A discussion requires two opinions."

"An opinion laced with lies doesn't count."

"But if you—"

"Silence!"

His shout echoed off the prison walls. Her stomach churned, but she clamped her lips shut.

"Now," he said, lower in pitch, "listen and learn. A traitor can challenge the king's reach, but only a fool underestimates mine. My men know this. Legions of Saracens—alive and dead—know it. Wulfstan will know it too."

"What has Wulfstan to do with this?"

William grunted. "You play innocence well."

"Truly, I know not whereof you speak!"

"I speak of your escape…tonight…with Wulfstan."

"What?"

"My squire was in the mews while you were plotting your little scheme."

"Holy Mother!" Emma cried. Frantically, her mind snatched up the pieces of what was said and where. "'Twas Gertrude's idea."

"A welcome one, reportedly."

"I considered it, but—"

"So you confess."

"No! Your spy heard but part of the conversation. In the end, I chose you."

William snorted. "Right. And I sell genuine relics of the saints."

Emma glared at him. With quick, deliberate steps, she closed the space between them.

"Then I'll fetch my purse," she said, "for I speak the truth."

"I am no fool."

No, she thought, *but you're a veritable god of arrogance.*

A lord of intimidation, too. Why else would he summon her to the prison tower? With dispatch, her desire to explain the curse, and its implications to their wedding night, died.

For an instant so brief she might've imagined it, his expression changed. He looked almost…wounded.

"Does the thought of marrying me so disgust you?" he asked.

His dark, infinite eyes became her world. "Not at all," she said.

Large, warm hands clasped her upper arms. "Is Wulfstan your lover?"

"No."

"Liar."

"Tyrant."

His mouth claimed hers. She wrenched her head to the side, tried to break away. His grip tightened. His lips demanded more.

Emma thought fast. She couldn't match his

physical strength. But maybe, if she didn't resist, didn't react in any way, he'd release her.

She willed herself to relax. Almost at once, his lips slackened. They became softer, gentler. Intrigued, she relaxed further.

His lips brushed hers and left a tingling warmth in their wake. She liked the sensation, but the longer he fed it, the more she wanted the full pressure of his mouth. A low sound of protest vibrated deep in her throat.

William moaned, and his hot tongue nudged her closed lips. To her, it seemed a curious action. Not unpleasant, though, so she opened her mouth. His tongue slipped inside and began a slow, thorough exploration. In response, she flicked her tongue against his.

He groaned. The sound was raw, exciting. His hands burned a path from her arms down to her hips. His tongue darted deeper, faster. Her mouth tingled. Heat tantalized her belly. Never had she felt so alive.

A fierce pounding at the chamber door broke the spell. Brusquely, William released her. A little off-balance, she straightened her spine and smoothed her tunic.

"Enter," William commanded.

The door swung open. Robert stepped inside and looked from William to Emma.

Her cheeks might as well have been aflame. Could Robert tell, simply by looking at them, what occurred in his absence?

Robert studied her for a moment, then regarded his brother. "The watchman spotted riders," he reported. "Two men approaching from the north."

"Our wedding guests?" William questioned.

"It appears so," Robert replied.

"Their timing is extraordinary," William muttered.

Emma snuck a glance at William. His expression was unreadable, and she could only assume his relentless will had conquered both his thoughts and his countenance. But she hadn't imagined his passionate kiss. Her lips still tingled.

The storm had passed. Yet she had no clue whether William believed her or not.

"Everything's in order," Robert continued. "I trust you've resolved your business here."

William turned to Emma, and his black eyes held a glint of humor. "I'm satisfied...for the moment," he said. Then he offered her his arm. "Shall we greet our guests?"

She hesitated, then placed her hand on his arm. His heat crept into her fingers and insinuated itself into her being.

Ignore it, she told herself. "Aye," she said aloud.

Together, they started toward the stairs and left the prison behind.

****

William hardly noticed the complex marriage of noise and efficiency transforming the great hall for the evening's feast. The army of busy servants seemed insignificant while his whole being honed in on the gentle pressure of Emma's hand on his arm.

The kiss had confirmed one truth: the lady was a passionate creature. She might dispute her involvement with Wulfstan, but she couldn't deny her carnal instincts. The thought that she might've tested those instincts on the Saxon swine burned through William's mind like acid.

With practiced discipline, he replaced the thought with logic and observation. He was no stranger to sexual pleasure, neither in the giving nor the taking of it. His experience suggested that Emma was innocent of a man's touch. She and Wulfstan might share an attraction, but William doubted she'd acted upon it.

Either that or Wulfstan is a blundering idiot, William mused. *An inept boy in the art of passion.*

The idea cheered William as he and Emma followed Robert into the keep's forebuilding. He nearly smiled at the guards flanking the small enclosure, until he recalled his response to the kiss. Emma had inspired in him a need that was unprecedented and disturbing.

Outside, the sound of horse hooves clopping over the drawbridge underscored a horn's expectant blare. There was no time to brood now. The brothers of Nihtscua had arrived.

Emma's fingers twitched on William's arm.

"Are you well, my lady?" he asked.

Emma took a deep breath. "Very well."

William wasn't convinced, but their guests awaited them. "Come," he said. With Robert to his right and Emma to his left, he stepped out onto the broad landing above the entrance stairs.

Below in the sunlit bailey, Aldred the Merciless stared up at the trio with eyes the color of shallow ice. His blond hair and beard created a flaming mane which did nothing to soften the harsh angles of his cheekbones and brow. Clad in crimson, he was a livid, glaring figure. He wore no mail, no sword. Only a scowl that vanished once he realized he was under scrutiny.

Wulfstan wore blue. He was clean-shaven, and like

his brother, he was tall, broad-shouldered, and blond. He too had ice blue eyes, yet his gaze was milder than Aldred's. To William, they were strangers, but there was no mistaking which man was which.

As a groom led their horses to the stable, Aldred and Wulfstan crossed the courtyard. At the same time, William, Emma, and Robert descended the wide, stone steps to the bailey floor.

"Aldred, Wulfstan." Emma smiled at each in turn. Her voice betrayed nothing of her dislike for the elder brother.

She is grace personified, William thought.

"My lady," Aldred said curtly.

Wulfstan regarded her with a warm gaze. "Emma."

William's eyes narrowed. He noticed a thick, horizontal scar above Wulfstan's left eye, and the imperfection pleased him.

"My bridegroom, Sir William," Emma continued smoothly, "and his brother, Sir Robert."

A quick succession of bowed heads and hooded glances followed the introduction.

Aldred's icy gaze stabbed William with its intensity. "We meet at last."

William's black eyes gave as good as they got. "'Tis our pleasure to welcome you and your brother on this momentous occasion," he said.

Aldred didn't blink. "Most everything you do is momentous. And though Ravenwood has always welcomed us, I thank you for the sentiment."

Had William worn his sword, he might've drawn it. "Sentiment plays no part here," he said tightly.

"All that matters is your comfort," Emma added in an obvious attempt to save the situation.

Wulfstan joined in her effort. "Gracious as always," he said, smiling. "It's been too long, Emma."

"It has indeed," she replied. "How fares your sister?"

"Well enough," Wulfstan answered.

"Little Freya must be nigh eight by now," she said.

"Nine."

"And prettier every day, I imagine."

Wulfstan grinned. "She may even outshine you one day."

Emma laughed, and the sound resembled that of a perfectly tuned bell. "That shouldn't be difficult!"

William observed the exchange with growing impatience. Their bond was both visible and vexing.

"Still modest, I see," Aldred cut in.

Emma stiffened. "You flatter me."

"Hardly," said Aldred. His cold gaze raked over her body.

Fury seared William's nerves. But he felt Robert's eyes on him, willing him to check his temper.

William spoke calmly, distinctly. "We offer our hospitality during your brief stay. See that you don't abuse it."

Aldred looked smug. "You would teach manners to me?"

"If need be," said William.

Wulfstan glanced at his brother. "There will be no need."

"Oh, I think 'the Storm' and I could learn a great deal from one another," Aldred said.

Robert spoke up. "What marvelous counsel could you give my brother?"

Aldred grinned. "You'd be surprised."

Robert clenched his fists. "I don't like surprises."

Aldred shrugged. "Pity."

"Welladay," Emma said quickly, "I'm sure you both want to get settled. John has made all of the arrangements. Shall we go find him?"

"Aye," said Wulfstan.

Aldred said nothing.

Emma looked up at William, and a silent plea ruled her features. "You needn't trouble yourself over these matters," she said. "I'll take our guests inside."

William nearly objected, but he saw the wisdom in it. A cooling-off period would benefit them all. "As you wish, my lady."

Emma's shoulders relaxed as she turned back to their guests. "If you'll accompany me."

Aldred and Wulfstan followed her up the steps. William watched their retreating forms, then turned to his brother.

"God's teeth!" Robert said under his breath.

"Quite," said William.

"You did well to control yourself."

"As did you, Robert."

"I must say I share the lady's preference for the younger brother."

William frowned. "'Tis difficult to choose between serpent and dragon."

"And how did Lady Emma defend her dragon?"

"With denials."

"Geoffrey heard her."

"She claims the plan was Gertrude's idea and that she rejected it."

"Do you believe her?"

"I believe a dragon has many scales."

Robert nodded. "We should keep an eye on him."

William stared at the archway through which the three Saxons disappeared. "We'll keep our eyes on them all."

Chapter Six

Seated at the high table in the great hall, Emma groaned inwardly. Supper was usually a modest, light repast, a chance to unwind after a busy day. Tonight was quite the opposite. Two feasts had been planned: the first, this evening, to honor their guests; then another, grander banquet to follow the wedding ceremony tomorrow. All of Ravenwood was welcome, from within the keep and without, and she found some comfort watching the familiar faces delight over numerous courses of costly, spiced foods. But while those at the lower tables reveled in rare delicacies and swayed to the lively music drifting down from the minstrel's gallery, the high table was grim.

The entire evening had seemed a silent battle between two pairs of brothers, Saxon and Norman. A ridiculous contest of surreptitious glances and warning glares. Caught in the middle, Emma felt like a prize pigeon.

Luckily, Gertrude had occupied Aldred for most of the meal. Now, he stood abruptly and left the hall. He should've taken his leave of both Emma and William, but Aldred rarely succumbed to the rules of polite society.

God be praised, Emma thought. She was in no mood to play the hostess for him.

"Good riddance," William muttered beside her.

Emma didn't know if he'd meant her to hear the comment, but she couldn't help agreeing. "Too right," she said.

He turned his black eyes on her as a cupbearer refilled his goblet with warm, mulled wine. "Do I detect a note of displeasure?"

She wrinkled her nose. "If I weren't a lady, you'd hear a screech of disgust."

His lips twitched as he poised his bejeweled dagger above a platter of roast mutton. "Shall I cut you more meat?"

"Only if I may then borrow your dagger for a more sinister deed."

He chuckled. "And I thought you welcomed our guests."

"One maybe."

All warmth fled from his eyes as they focused on the sole Saxon male remaining at table. She followed his stare. Gertrude now showered her attention on Wulfstan.

Emma took a deep breath. "Sir William," she said in a voice louder than she'd intended.

His gaze reclaimed hers.

"I spoke true this afternoon," she said.

William studied her in silence. His razor-sharp focus sucked unwelcome heat into her cheeks.

"Then why do you blush?" he asked.

"Because you're eyeing me as a cat would a cornered mouse."

"Are you cornered, my lady?"

"'Tis your game. You tell me."

"I play no game. My intentions are plain, and the king approves them. 'Tis you who have plotted and schemed since my arrival."

"Do you truly believe I have naught better to do than conspire against you?"

"How can I believe otherwise?"

"A tiny thing called trust."

"My trust isn't given freely. It must be earned."

She glared at him. "At what cost?"

Suddenly, Gertrude was beside her. "You're needed in the kennel." Her voice held a note of urgency.

Emma looked up at her. "What is it?"

"Thomas just informed me that one of the greyhounds was injured in the hunt," Gertrude explained. "They've tried to mend its leg, but the poor thing is in terrible pain."

Emma's stomach heaved. She'd been so rapt in her argument with William, she'd not even seen the huntsman's apprentice. She stood up. "I must help."

William regarded her through narrowed eyes. "I'll send Robert with you."

Emma turned toward Robert. He and Wulfstan were engaged in an animated discussion. Although neither man smiled, they were communicating. She wouldn't jeopardize the small miracle.

"Let him enjoy the feast," she said. "I'll work fast and return anon."

William hesitated, then gave her a nod. "We'll wait for you."

"Thank you. And Gertrude, you needn't leave the hall either."

Emma hurried along the dais, down the steps, and out of the hall, leaving the cacophony of laughter, toasts, and soaring flutes behind her. Then she flew to the bailey. Shivering without her mantle, she scurried across the courtyard to the long, wooden façade of the kennel. She threw open the door and rushed inside.

All was still. She glanced around the dimly lit interior. The castle dogs stirred in the fresh straw and watched her with tails wagging.

Behind her, the kennel door creaked shut. Slowly, she turned.

Aldred blocked the door. The rush-lighting flickered, conjuring strange, inhuman shadows which slithered along the peaks and hollows of his face.

"Alone at last," he hummed.

A slight quiver ran through her. "Where's Thomas? Where's—"

"There's no one here but us," he said, leering at her. "Everyone is feasting and belching away in the hall."

The truth dawned, and she gritted her teeth. "There is no wounded greyhound."

"Smart girl. Don't be angry with Gertrude. She only wanted to help."

Right, Emma thought. *All she's done is help since this nightmare began.*

Aloud, she said, "I suppose you think you're clever, luring me here with lies."

"Whatever works, my dear."

"I am not your dear."

"A minor point. Especially when it can be rectified so easily."

"By the saints! Is that what this is about?"

"The saints have no say in the matter. Nor has Sir William. If you want freedom from his Norman vise, all you need do is ask."

"And exchange one vise for another? I think not."

"That's your problem. You don't think. You're ready to hand over Saxon land on a golden plate! If your father were alive—"

"He'd be nursing his eternal hatred for the invaders and supporting another Saxon uprising or Scottish plot."

"He was a great man!"

"He was a menace. And he's dead, Aldred. I follow the king's desires now."

"Desires? What do you know of those?"

She frowned. "Speak plainly."

His eyes blazed. "You'll spread your legs in a Norman bed while your black knight sows his rotten seed. And you'll scream and weep and wish you'd accepted me instead."

She stepped backward. "You're mad."

"Not so," he spat. "I'm the only one who can satisfy you. I know your desires, even if you don't."

"Do not think to pollute my desires with the likes of yours."

"Oh, you've no idea, witch. There's a fine line between pleasure and pain, and I can teach it to you."

She gagged. Some of the hounds began to growl.

"Think of it, Emma. The Norman's head on a spike. Me as master of Ravenwood. And you tied to our bed, shrieking with the ecstasy found only on the other side of torture."

She curled her fingers into tight fists. "Get out of my sight," she ordered.

A gurgling sound that approximated laughter erupted from his throat. "Are you threatening me?"

"With every drop of strength I possess."

"And how much is that? Shall we test it and see?"

The kennel now seethed with growls and bared teeth as an army of hounds smelled conflict.

Emma lifted her chin. "If you persist in this vein, I'll tell my bridegroom of your proposals. Then we'll see what kind of test he can devise."

Aldred's smirk became a scowl. "Very well," he said, "but you'll regret this."

"My only regret is that I've allowed you to defile my wedding."

"By what means? My superior claim to your hand?"

"No, by your mere attendance."

His eyes narrowed. "So Ravenwood's kennel boasts a new bitch."

Emma pointed to the door, then injected her voice with as much poison as she could rouse. "Out!"

****

William soundlessly melded with the shadows of the east tower. Alert for any hint of movement, his gaze combed the length of the kennel from a distance of twenty yards. He'd left Robert in the hall, ordering him with a glance to keep an eye on Wulfstan. Robert wouldn't disappoint. He'd cling to the Saxon's movements like a second skin.

Shrouded in darkness and inured to the cold, William waited. The black sky was pitted with stars that glittered like the pieces of an unsolvable puzzle.

Emma seemed genuinely concerned when summoned to the kennel. Yet Geoffrey had overheard her plotting to escape. Tonight. Aldred left the hall just minutes before she did. There had to be a connection.

The kennel door swung open. Aldred stormed out

61

and slammed the door behind him. Grumbling to himself like a seasoned curmudgeon, he stomped toward the keep.

William waited until Aldred disappeared around the corner. Then he made his move. Silently, he crept to the kennel door and listened. There was only a slight rustle of straw within, so he opened the door.

"Are you deaf?" Emma said. "I told you to leave."

Seated on the kennel floor, she stared at the small, black spaniel cradled in her lap. The soft light caressed her stormy features like a silent prayer. For peace? That would be found only on the other side of their wedding.

He stepped inside and shut the door behind him. "Did you, now?"

Emma looked up with wide, beautiful eyes. "Sir William! I thought you were—"

"Aldred," he finished. "I give you leave to rejoice."

"Rejoice?"

"That 'tis I in his stead."

Her smile was cautious. "'Tis an improvement, I admit."

He scanned the kennel. "Where's the wounded greyhound?"

"There is none."

"I guessed as much."

She made a face. "I wish I had. Perhaps I'm too willing to trust. But I came hither because I cannot bear the thought of others in pain."

"If that's a flaw, 'tis a noble one."

She beamed at him, and the act seemed to brighten the entire building. "Was that a compliment?"

He grinned. "Aye."

"'Twas well worth the wait, if I may say so."

"You may."

"And may I also ask you to sit down? Your height is a definite asset, but my neck is beginning to ache."

He couldn't help but smile as he squatted and settled on the ground across from her. "Better?"

"Much," she said. "You could certainly give Aldred a lesson in manners."

William snapped a piece of straw between his fingers. "Did he insult you again?"

"Only with words."

"Threats?"

"Empty ones."

"His reputation was built on deeds, not words."

"True, but everyone is against him. You, your brother, the king. Even Wulfstan."

His handful of straw died with a loud crunch. "You assume a lot. Or has Wulfstan told you this?"

"He doesn't need to. His relationship with Aldred has always been strained."

"I see."

"I hope you do," she said pointedly. "Wulfstan isn't your enemy."

"How do you know?"

She heaved a sigh. "I feel it."

He threw the crushed straw onto the floor. "Does Wulfstan always inspire such feeling in you?"

"What if he does?"

"Answer the question."

"Of course I have feelings for him. We've been friends a long time."

"Only friends?"

"Why should you care?"

William wondered the same thing. "I must guard

my interests."

Emma dropped her gaze to the puppy and began to stroke its belly. "Right," she said. "That's all I am. An interest. Chattel."

He watched the smooth, rhythmic motions of her hand. She'd favored Thunder with the same gentle touch. "I meant no disrespect."

"I know," she murmured, her head bowed, her eyes downcast.

A rush of tenderness seized him. He leaned over and brushed her forehead with a feather-soft kiss.

Her lips parted. They were full, luscious, and as sweet a temptation as he'd ever known.

The spaniel in her lap let out a high-pitched whine. Emma giggled, but her cheeks flared with color when the puppy burrowed against her and sniffed her crotch.

"Oh no, you don't," she said. In one quick motion, she scooped him up and stood. Then she bent over a stall and placed him inside it. "Back to bed. You've had enough petting for one night."

The curve of Emma's backside was like a beacon. William got to his feet and stole toward her. Desire coursed through his veins, and his body heat devoured the chill in the surrounding air.

Emma straightened and turned. Then she jumped at the sight of him standing so close. "You have a gift for sneaking up on people."

He moved closer and stopped mere inches away. Her hair smelled sweet and held a hint of roses. 'Twas a pity she'd have to cover it with a veil once they were married.

He nodded toward the puppy. "How do you know he's had enough petting?"

Her reply sounded breathless. "I just do."

"That's not an answer. Do you know why he sniffed you?"

"All dogs do it. Their sense of smell is precise, and it makes them curious."

"But with such precision, there must've been a reason why he nuzzled you just now."

"What reason?"

"He sensed the change in your scent after I kissed you."

Her eyes widened. "What change?"

"I think you know."

"I think you're rude."

"Let's just say, I'm perceptive."

"There was no change in me."

"Would you mind if I verified that?" He bent down as if to repeat the dog's action.

She gripped his shoulders and tried to push him away. "I certainly would!"

Grinning, he straightened. "Since you're so unwilling, I must be right."

"You wouldn't attempt such a thing in the light of day."

"Wouldn't I?"

"The sun would show your every move."

"Since when do you crave the sun? I thought you favored storms."

"I do."

"Then drink of mine."

Emma backed into a thick, oak beam. Recovering quickly, she squared her shoulders and lifted her chin. "You're a bold one."

William closed the distance between them. "A

warrior cannot afford to be timid."

"We are not engaged in battle."

"But we are engaged to be wed." His gaze lowered to her tunic's skirt. "At least part of you welcomes me."

She stiffened. "Don't celebrate your victory just yet."

"You're right, my lady. We'll do that tomorrow night."

A shiver racked her body. He stepped forward and slid his arms around her waist. Her scent was intoxicating.

"You're cold," he said, bowing his head. Her plump, ripe lips were but a breath away. "Let me warm you."

His mouth found hers. Her lips were warm and yielding, a delicacy to be savored. He teased them open with his tongue and probed gently, tasting her sweetness with slow, lingering movements. Her tongue slid along his and joined in a delicate duel of taste and texture.

His hands roamed her tunic, molding the soft fabric to her waist, hips, and buttocks. He squeezed her bottom and pulled her close so she could feel the full length of his arousal.

She tore her mouth from his. "Sir!"

His lips traveled to her right ear. "My lady," he whispered.

She trembled. He felt the small quake as though 'twere his own.

"Still cold?" he teased. His teeth grazed her earlobe.

Again, she shivered. "I…"

His tongue traced her silken flesh, down the length

of her neck. His right hand slid upward and cupped a breast. With light, measured strokes, his thumb caressed her through the tunic.

He grinned as the nipple hardened beneath the cloth. He himself was hard as steel.

"You like that?" he whispered against the hollow of her throat.

She shuddered.

"Yet you shiver from cold," he said. "How ever shall I warm you?"

He blazed a trail of hot kisses from the base of her throat down to the breast cupped in his palm. Gently, his teeth skimmed the linen that shielded the rigid pap.

"I-I'm not cold," she stammered.

He tweaked her nipple. "But your teat points straight as an arrow."

"And you know why," she said in a thick voice.

"So do you," he said, straightening.

Her eyes had become dark pools of passion. Her body was lush and inviting. But this was neither the time nor the place.

With a sigh, he pulled away. "'Tis late."

"And tomorrow will be a long day," she added.

"Tonight will be longer."

She inched out from between his body and the wooden beam. "Tilda must be waiting to see me to bed."

He grinned. "'Twill soon be our bed."

She avoided his gaze. "I must go."

"As you wish," he said. "Until tomorrow."

Emma stumbled to the door and jerked it open. She turned and regarded him once more. "Tomorrow."

Chapter Seven

At daybreak, Emma climbed the small hill to Woden's Circle. Pervasive fog seemed to cushion her feet and blur her conflicting emotions. She was all too glad to let reality fade into the mist behind her. Truth be told, a part of her wanted to keep walking until she disappeared into the swirling fog. Forever.

The stone ring was pagan in origin. Perhaps 'twould swallow her up and whisk her to an enchanted, parallel world. A fairyland where she could forget duty and curses, and her beguiling, dangerous bridegroom.

In a way, he was just as magical as the stones atop the mound. He teased, mesmerized, and wove a sticky web of seduction. In both the prison and the kennel, he'd made her forget herself.

That was the one thing she could never do.

Emma crested the hill and entered the towering circle. Then she stepped inside the gateway at its core. Already, her raven guardians had gathered, perched *en masse* on the ancient stones.

She closed her eyes, stretched out her arms, and touched the cold, gray stones. Her prayer was a single word. "Please."

The ground and stones thrummed with energy, and the vision came, just as before. Violet eyes. Margaret's troubled expression. Her swollen belly. Her finger pointing to what waited beyond.

Emma turned and peered through the mist. She saw herself, lying in bed.

Her body lay abnormally still. Her face was an ashen shell. She was dead.

Horror ripped her from the vision. She slapped a hand to her chest, and her quick, strong heartbeats reassured her. Breathing deeply, she wiped the sweat from her brow.

The message seemed clear: if she became pregnant, she would die. 'Twas the curse's terrible promise.

"As if I need reminding," she muttered.

"What you need is a watchdog."

Emma whirled around. "Meg, what are you doing here?"

With her long veil and flowing, white tunic, Meg seemed an extension of the enveloping mist. "I could ask the same of you. And today of all days."

"Why should today be any different?"

"'Tis your wedding day!"

Emma threw her hands in the air. "And already, 'tis ripe with useless reminders."

"What has you in so foul a temper?" Meg asked.

"Let me see," said Emma. "I live under a curse. I suffer Aldred's putrid presence. I've just had a terrifying vision. And today I marry a conceited Norman who's little more than a stranger. Take your pick."

Meg's violet eyes were as shrewd as her wit. "I'll choose the third complaint, if I may."

Emma's shoulders slumped. "I saw my mother again. She wants me to heed the curse."

"Mayhap she wants you to break it."

"And how would I do that?"

"You know how. With true love."

Emma snorted. "Have you seen any lately?"

"Not yet, child."

"Not ever, you mean."

Meg folded her arms. "'Tis unlike you to be so negative."

Tears pricked Emma's eyes, but she blinked them away. "I know. I'm sorry."

"Don't apologize. Just have hope."

"I might if Sir William were capable of love."

"Why do you think he's not?"

Emma's mind flooded with images: Sir William summoning her to the prison tower; his black eyes gleaming with suspicion in the hall; the way he'd teased her in the kennel, as if he knew exactly how to drown her in a sensuality she dared not embrace.

"He's cold and calculating...and unbelievably stingy with his trust," she said at last.

"You're out of breath," Meg remarked.

I am, Emma realized. Her emotions had so entangled her that she was panting like a puppy. What was next?

"Believe me," she said, "Sir William is hopeless."

Meg looked thoughtful. "I've known many a worse case."

She was right, of course. One had only to imagine Aldred as a bridegroom to learn the definition of hopelessness.

All at once, Emma's mood broke. She pushed her shoulders back and stood a little straighter. "Did you follow me here?"

"No. I was restless. So I came to be with the ravens and the spirits...and the wind that carries them."

Emma understood. Age, beauty, mystery, and might coexisted within the stone ring. Its magic, and the souls who'd experienced it, were timeless.

"I wish I'd known my mother," she said softly.

Meg patted Emma's arm. "She was a passionate woman, and though she feared the curse, she wanted you desperately. Perhaps that's why her love reaches out to you, even now."

"As a warning."

"As a blessing."

"I'd feel better if she were with me today."

"She will be. You'll be wearing her gown."

"That I will. 'Tis amazing how well it fits. Tilda made only a few alterations."

"You'll be beautiful."

"I'll be petrified."

Meg chuckled. "Try to relax. Stress only clouds the mind. Let's go back to the keep and break our fast."

They left the circle and started down the hill. The fog began to dissipate.

"We've a busy day ahead," Meg said.

Emma rolled her eyes. "And an eventful night, no doubt. At least Sir William agreed that we should withdraw to our chamber alone after the festivities."

"Without witnesses? Your guests will be disappointed."

"What I must tell my husband is private, and we'll serve enough wine and ale to drown any objections."

Meg nodded. "'Twill be easier if you're alone."

"Easier, but not easy."

"I know, but don't spoil the day by fretting about tonight. When the time comes, your heart will guide you."

"I'd rather my head did."

"The heart is wiser."

"Explain that to the curse."

Meg paused and laid a hand on Emma's cheek. "No," she said, her violet eyes dark with emotion. "You must explain the curse to your husband."

****

The lord's private chapel was the most beautiful place in the castle. As William awaited his bride before the altar, he studied the small chamber.

The ceiling and walls had been carved and painted with artistic grace seldom seen outside royal households. The altar was draped with shining, white satin. Its centerpiece was an enormous gold cross, flanked by two, large beeswax candles in gold candlesticks. Behind the altar, a single arched window fcaturcd costly glass stained in blue, green, and red. No one who entered the chapel would question the wealth of Ravenwood's lord.

He'd abandoned his customary black attire for blue. 'Twasn't an easy choice. Blue was a symbol of purity, and he'd sinned enough in his lifetime to make the color shrink from his flesh. Still, the tunic was embroidered with silver thread, and a jewel-studded belt was the perfect complement. 'Twas his finest court apparel and the only clothing worthy of the occasion.

Emma had insisted that Wulfstan give her away. William had agreed, though the compromise was as palatable as sour wine.

But Lady Emma will be mine by the end of the hour, he thought. *After that, Wulfstan can go to the Devil. Who knows? Satan's company might be a welcome respite from Aldred's.*

He glanced at Robert, who stood tall and stoic at his side. Robert's gaze roved about the chapel.

He's assessing the riches into which I marry, just as Aldred is gauging his losses.

The Saxon's scowl was as fervent now as when he first entered the chapel. Gertrude, who looked equally grim, sat beside him on the bench. The only smile in the room belonged to Meg. Her countenance was as serene and lovely as the chapel itself, and something in the tilt of her head reminded William of Emma.

The next instant, he needed no reminder. Emma crossed the chapel's threshold on Wulfstan's arm, and William forgot about Ravenwood's wealth and the horror of battles past. All he could see was his bride.

She glided toward the altar with the poise of a queen. She wore lavender silk and a fine, richly embroidered veil over her hair. Amethysts and rubies dotted a silver belt which accentuated her waist and hips and trailed down the front of her skirt in one long, shimmering line.

Her violet eyes sparkled as she approached the altar. In that moment, she embodied all that was good and the essence of desire. She resembled the haunting beauty of a storm. His storm.

He chafed at Wulfstan's presence. But before he knew it, Father Cedric bent his shiny bald head over the prayer book and began the ceremony.

"Beloved brethren..." the chaplain intoned.

Beloved, William mused. *By whom? God? Each other?*

The only evidence he'd seen of real love between a man and woman was the bond his parents had shared. His mother, though strong and proud, still mourned her husband's death.

Would anyone mourn his? Although he'd bedded many women, he'd entrusted his heart only to one. That had been the mistake of his life, one he'd paid for, body and soul.

"Sir William," said Father Cedric, "will you take this woman as your wife, and love and honor her, guard her and keep her in health and sickness, as it befits a husband should do his wife, and forsaking all others for her sake, stay only with her all the days you both shall live?"

William sobered. He could never love Emma, but he would strive to uphold the other vows. "I will," he said.

Father Cedric turned to Emma and asked her the same. William held his breath.

"I will," she said in a strong, clear voice.

He relaxed. Beside him, Wulfstan placed Emma's right hand in the priest's. With the formal betrothal complete, Wulfstan and Robert joined the other three guests on the bench. Then Father Cedric motioned for William to take Emma's right hand.

Her fingers were ice-cold. He willed his warmth into them as the chaplain continued with the ceremony.

Her voice was softer, less certain, as she repeated her vows. "I, Emma, take thee, William, to my wedded husband, to have and to hold, for better, for worse, for richer, for poorer, in sickness and in health…"

Her voice trailed into silence for one heart-stopping moment. Then she squared her shoulders and continued, "To be bonny and buxom in bed and at board, to love and to cherish, till death us depart, if holy Church will it ordain, and thereto I plight thee my troth."

Father Cedric blessed the simple gold band which lay on his prayer book, then handed it to William.

"With this ring, I thee wed," William said. "With my body I thee worship, and with all my worldly chattel I thee honor."

He pushed the ring onto Emma's thumb. "*In nomine Patris*," he stated. He moved the ring to her index finger. "*Et Filii*," he said, then placed the ring on her third finger, saying, "*et Spiritus Sancti*." Finally, he slid the ring on her fourth finger. "Amen."

She avoided his gaze as they knelt before the priest to receive the blessing. Only when they rose to leave did she look up at him. Her eyes were dark with emotions and thoughts he couldn't read, but he squeezed her hand to reassure her. She gave him a closed-mouth smile, and he grinned in return. Her hand was now warm and accepting.

Together, they turned and strode from the altar. The puckered brows of Aldred and Gertrude were like a chorus of disapproval, but Meg's eyes glistened with unshed tears. Both Robert and Wulfstan smiled at the couple.

Once outside the sanctum, William sighed and glanced at his bride. It felt almost natural to walk beside her.

"That wasn't so bad, was it?" he asked.

"No...my lord," she said. "Quite lovely, in fact."

"'Tis you who are lovely," he said before he could stop himself.

Her cheeks colored. "Another compliment? Take care, or I shall swoon."

"Not until bedtime," he warned playfully.

Her smile disappeared.

"Fear not," he whispered. "I won't bite."

"Your teeth don't concern me," she muttered. "I'm sure you've a much sharper weapon at your command."

William laughed. He felt happier than he had in months. He was Lord Ravenwood now, and his lady embodied wit and beauty.

"Come," he said as they approached the arched entrance to the great hall. "All of Ravenwood awaits us."

The newlyweds entered the hall to the fanfare of trumpets. The people shouted and cheered, and William proudly led Emma onto the dais and to their seats at the high table.

A moment later, Meg, Gertrude, Wulfstan, and Robert joined them. Pages stepped forward with ewers, basins, and napkins.

As William washed his hands, he turned to Robert. "Where's Aldred?" he asked in a low voice.

"Gone," Robert replied.

"What?"

"True to form, he flouts custom and decency. I suppose he couldn't stomach the celebration, now that the marriage is well and truly sealed."

"Did he give any excuse?"

"None. He simply announced he was leaving."

"Well, that's one Saxon boil off my skin."

"Only one. Wulfstan intends to stay a few days."

William rolled his eyes as he dried his hands. "Of course he does."

"Don't worry," Robert said with a grin. "I'll keep an eye on him."

"Good. Your eye is as keen as they come."

"Keen enough to detect a change in you."

"What change?"

Robert ran his hand along the smooth, white tablecloth. "Well, for a start, you just complimented me."

William grunted. "'Tis the second compliment I've offered today. I must be losing my touch."

"Or your heart?"

William's mood soured. "Never," he vowed. Then a slight pressure on his forearm drew his attention.

"My lord." Emma removed her hand from his arm. "Is aught amiss?"

"No," Robert said quickly. "What could be amiss on so fine a day?"

William gave his brother a meaningful look. Then he turned to his bride. "What indeed?"

"I'm glad to hear it," she said. "You'll need your appetite for the feast we've planned."

Suddenly, William forgot Robert's comment. Lavender silk consumed his focus.

"I can assure you," he murmured, "I'm ravenous."

Chapter Eight

The wedding feast went on and on. The guests ate pheasants, peacocks, partridges, and quails. Goose, heron, venison, and rabbit. There were eel pies, fruit tarts, eggs, and custards. With each course came a subtlety, a sugar and marzipan model of a castle or boat. Always, there was more ale, and more warm, spiced wine.

Toasts abounded, and the music soared. Yet Emma's gaze kept straying to the gold ring on her finger. 'Twas tangible proof she was a married woman, the property of William l'Orage. Soon, in the bedchamber they would share, she'd discover exactly what that meant.

She shuddered. Would he understand her predicament? He might laugh. He might even force her to betray her sense of self preservation. 'Twas his right, and she'd said the words: "to be bonny and buxom in bed and at board." The board she could handle; bed was another matter.

Still, there were moments during the ceremony when he seemed softer somehow. When she entered the chapel, the look in his eyes stole her breath. It implied approval, pride.

And desire.

For the second time in as many minutes, she shivered. She looked to the high, vaulted ceiling and twisted her wedding band.

"Cold again?" her husband asked. The low, rich timbre of his voice was seductive and becoming all too familiar.

She dropped her hands into her lap and cast a cautious glance his way. "Not especially."

A pox on the man! He looked sinfully handsome today. It made him unduly appealing and far more dangerous. His eyes glittered like the dark jewels on his belt.

She squirmed in her high-backed chair. *His belt,* she thought. *God save me from what lies below it.*

"You'll be warmer once we withdraw to our chamber," he said.

She swallowed the lump in her throat. "Oh?"

"I told Tilda to have a fire waiting, and plenty of warm wine."

"Oh."

"Is that all you can say?"

"What more do you require?"

"If not words, how about a smile?"

"I've smiled overmuch the past few hours. My cheeks are numb."

His grin was sensual by nature and mischievous by design. "Have you no enthusiasm for the coming festivities?"

She stifled a grimace. "Festivities," she said. "Is that what you call them? If you want a festive night, you'd do better to invite jugglers and mummers to prance about the chamber."

His black eyes smoldered. "No, my bride. You and I will devise our own entertainment."

The power of speech deserted her. Yet she kept her

composure during the toasts and as the people cheered the bride and groom for the last time. Then William rose to his feet.

The dreaded moment had come. In a daze, she stood. Her eyes sought Meg, but the older woman was deep in conversation with Wulfstan and didn't notice.

William guided Emma away from the table and out of the boisterous, oblivious hall. Once they were beyond observation, she pulled her hand from his arm and used her veil as an excuse to occupy her hands elsewhere.

She climbed the spiral, stone stairs as slowly as she dared, delaying the moment when the bedchamber door would close behind them. The stairwell torches were ablaze with flames that eagerly licked the shafts of wood. Behind her, William's footsteps were as loud as thunder.

At the top of the stairs, the large, oak door stood wide open. There was no one inside the bedchamber, not a single soul to grant her one last pardon. Tilda had turned down the bed, and it loomed in the shadows, waiting.

On shaky legs, Emma crossed the rush-strewn floor and stood in front of the massive, arched fireplace. She studied the inferno roaring inside, refusing to look at William. Behind her, the door closed with a thud, and the bolt slid to with a scrape of finality. She heard and felt each crunching step as he came up behind her.

"My lady," he murmured. "My wife."

She couldn't face him. "Aye," her voice cracked. The fire looked wild, hungry.

"Would you like some wine?" he asked.

His breath warmed the side of her neck. A second

later, his lips sealed the tender flesh with a kiss.

"Wine," she said, spinning around. "Wine would be nice."

His eyes blazed hotter than the fire. He hesitated, then smiled. "Then wine you shall have," he said, moving in two strides to the table where it waited. He grabbed the pitcher and poured dark liquid into one of two silver cups. Then he offered one to her.

Her fingers brushed his as she took the cup. She thanked him with a closed-mouth smile and took a sip of wine. The heady mixture of cinnamon, ginger, cardamom, nutmeg, and cloves tickled her tongue. The liquid warmed and soothed her throat.

"Good?" he said.

She nodded and sipped again.

He grinned. "Perhaps 'twill loosen your tongue."

"Perhaps."

His grin deepened. "Though I see it's had no effect yet."

Hours of nervous tension crystallized. "I've better use for my tongue than to prattle the night away."

"Really?" he said, stepping closer. "Would you care to demonstrate?"

The silver cup froze midway to her lips. "I didn't mean—"

"I know you didn't, but the idea has merit."

"The wine is delicious," she stalled. "Won't you have some?"

"I've had my fill."

She gulped down the rest of hers. "I could use another cup."

He stole the cup from her hand, placed it on the table, and returned without it. "You could use a kiss."

"No, I think—"

His lips silenced her. They were strong, demanding. A heartbeat later, she returned his kiss. She blamed the wine and silently scolded herself, even as her hands slipped up his chest and encircled his neck.

With a groan, he thrust his tongue into her mouth, and she received it, willingly. Her tongue toyed with his in a game of cat and mouse. Her fingers slid into his dark, silken hair, and she clung to him as the kiss swept her beyond sense and reason.

'Twas a tempest. 'Twas heaven.

His hands roved like the wind over her silk gown. His mouth rained hot kisses down her neck to the valley between her breasts. In another minute, she'd be gone, lost in a haze of sensation.

A warning bell clanged in her mind. She rallied every ounce of her strength and pulled away from him.

"I'm sorry," she said breathlessly.

His eyes shone like black onyx. "Emma."

'Twas the first time he'd addressed her so. No title. No pretense. Just her name.

"Forgive me," she said, "but I must speak to you."

He folded his arms. "Then speak."

No turning back now, she thought. *Here we go.*

She took a deep breath. "There's a matter of great importance that involves us both…well, all of Ravenwood, really. You see, there's a curse."

"I know."

Her mouth fell open. "How? When?"

"People gossip," he replied blandly.

She crossed her arms, mirroring his stance. "Mayhap you know what I'm about to say."

"If you're going to tell me the curse is nonsense,

then I applaud your intellect."

"'Tis not nonsense but very real. For centuries, every mistress of Ravenwood has died in childbirth."

"Coincidence."

She shook her head. "No, the curse."

"So say the peasants."

She bristled. "So say I."

He turned to the fireplace, and she took a step back. She held her breath as he stared into the flames.

At last, he regarded her. "You're not serious."

"Unfortunately, I am."

"Why do you mention this now?"

"Because there can be no wedding night. Not the kind you want."

His nostrils flared. "What I want is my right. I am your husband."

"I know that, but you must try to understand. If I become pregnant, I'll die."

"Ridiculous."

"I wish 'twere so."

"Ravenwood must have heirs."

"No matter the cost to me?"

"There will be no cost."

Her body shook. "There will!"

His arms dropped to his sides. "So what are you saying?"

"I'm saying that I'll be your loyal and obedient wife in all ways but one. You must never bed me."

He clenched his fists. "I see. Why didn't you tell me before the ceremony?"

"I was afraid."

"Of what?"

She sighed heavily. "You. Myself. Losing your

protection."

"Protection from whom? Aldred?"

"And his kind."

His eyes narrowed. "You would use me thus?"

Her hands found her hips. "You used me to gain land and position."

"And sons! Do you think Ravenwood and our other manors can survive without them?"

"You forget. Our union was the king's bidding, not mine."

"I forget nothing."

She threw her hands up. "Oh! First you fear nothing, and now you forget nothing. God himself must marvel at your perfection."

"As he must rue your disobedience," he said, stepping forward. "You made a vow."

"And now I must make a bargain."

"I don't bargain with liars."

"And I will not give my body to a man who cannot love!"

He reached out. His large hands clamped around her upper arms. "I could force you," he barked.

She lowered her gaze to the endless network of rushes on the floor. "You could," she murmured.

Abruptly, William released her and stomped to the door. He yanked the bolt free and twisted his head around. "Good night, Lady Ravenwood," he bit out. "May you rot in your damnable chastity!"

The heavy door slammed shut. Emma turned toward the bed and stared at its cold, linen sheets. Tears welled in her eyes. She'd never felt so alone.

****

The rest of the keep still rocked with merriment.

Careful to avoid the great hall, William stormed to the prison tower. At the bottom of the stairs, he snatched a torch from the wall.

He climbed the tower with a vengeance. His chest tightened a little more with each step. Once inside the prison chamber, he thrust the torch into an empty wall socket. Then he began to pace.

'Twas outrageous. Not to be borne! He'd faced pain, hardship, armies of Saracens salivating for the kill. Yet, on the other side of the keep, in his bedchamber, stood a mere slip of a girl who mocked everything for which he'd fought.

I should've expected betrayal, he thought. *Why should Emma be any different from—*

No! Years ago, he'd vowed never to say her name again, never to think it. The past was dead, buried.

The prison door swung open, and he whipped around. Robert stood at the threshold.

"Well?" William demanded.

Robert stared at him. "Well what?"

"Are you going to lurk on the doorsill all night or come in?"

Robert slipped into the chamber and closed the door behind him. "What," he said, pausing for emphasis, "are you doing here?"

"Ask my bride."

"I'm asking you."

William glared at the chamber's cold, empty fireplace. So like his wife. And his heart.

"William," said Robert.

Despite the chill in the room, sweat beaded on William's brow. "What?"

"Does this concern Wulfstan?"

William's temperature rose a notch. "Fortunately, no."

"I'm glad to hear it. If circumstances were different, we might actually be friends."

"You and Wulfstan?"

"Aye."

A rumble sounded deep in William's throat.

"Are you going to tell me why you're here?" Robert asked. "Or must I wait until we're old and gray?"

William strode to the fireplace, then back again. "You were right," he growled. "My wife does believe in the curse. She just told me."

"Ah. And how did that drive you to spend your wedding night in a prison?"

"The stench of merry-making plagues the rest of the keep, and I need peace."

"And 'twouldn't look right if Ravenwood's new lord were seen roaming about the castle when he should be enjoying the pleasures of his bed."

"We never made it to the bed."

"I see. So at present, Lady Ravenwood is scared of pregnancy."

"Not just scared. She refuses to consummate the marriage."

"Ever?"

"So she says."

"God's blood! 'Tis unthinkable!"

"My thoughts exactly."

"What will you do?"

"I don't know yet. I'm too furious to decide."

Robert's gray eyes widened. "You owe your success in battle to calm logic. Clear tactics. You don't let emotion dim your judgment. 'Tis why so many fear you."

William stared at the wall in front of him. The flaming torch created a miniature battle of shadows on stone. "I know," he muttered.

Robert rubbed his chin. Then he began to pace. His footfalls created a smooth, continuous rhythm on the planked floor. Suddenly, he stopped.

"We know the curse is codswallop," he said.

"Utterly," William agreed.

"Can you convince your wife of this?"

"Not before she survives the birthing bed."

Robert looked pensive and nodded slowly. "Then you must make her forget until that day arrives."

William grunted. "One might as soon make a knight forget his sword on the battlefield."

"Then coax her into choosing you in spite of her fears."

"You suggest a miracle."

"No," Robert said, shaking his head. He raised an eyebrow. "A seduction."

William regarded his brother in silence.

"I've seen your charm at work," Robert said. "You've lain with more women than I can count, and you've had every opportunity to perfect your lovemaking skills. I remember a certain sultan who rewarded your mercy with the use of his harem."

"An offer I could hardly refuse," William said, smiling. For a moment, he was back in the exotic East, surrounded by perfume, rare silks, and the tantalizing flesh of a sea of women.

"I doubt there's a maid alive who could resist you indefinitely, and Lady Ravenwood is your wife. She's legally bound to you. With time and persuasion, she'll give in."

William felt lighter, reassured. "Perhaps you're right. But for tonight, I'll stay here."

"And I'll stay with you. As prisons go, this one isn't half bad."

"A veritable palace."

"I wouldn't go that far."

"I would, but for one night only. My wife may deny me her body, but she'll not rob me of comfort."

"Nor should she. The bed is now yours."

"And I'll have her in it."

In a mock toast, Robert lifted his hand as though holding a goblet brimming with spirits. "She'll fawn over you with a saint's devotion."

"I want no saint in my bed."

"A wanton angel, then."

"That's better." William eyed the torch on the wall. He could feel its heat even from a distance.

Robert clapped him on the back. "'Twill happen, Brother. You'll see."

William grinned. "So shall Lady Ravenwood."

Chapter Nine

The wind moaned a woeful song the following morning. It woke Emma from a fitful sleep she was glad to forsake. Alone in the massive bed, she rolled onto her side and stared into the murky depths of the chamber. The fire had died in the night, and the oak shutters were still barred against the wind. Below, the castle stirred to life.

Memory inundated her with echoes of words and emotions. Her wedding night was a disaster, an experiment in shame. Regret rose in her throat. She'd said some hurtful things to William. She never intended to insult him, but she refused to sacrifice herself on the altar of his pride and lust.

Outside, the wind howled as though wounded.

I know, Emma thought. *I agree completely.*

Suddenly, she had to be a part of it: the wind, the world. She kicked off the covers and hopped out of bed. Shuddering against the cold, she rushed to one of the large chests lining the wall and threw open the lid. She grabbed a white tunic and slipped into it.

Three knocks sounded on the door, and Tilda's voice traveled through the thick oak. "My lady?"

Emma unbolted and opened the door. "Come in."

With a small oil lamp in hand, Tilda shuffled inside. Her gaze darted about the room. Then, hand on chest, she sighed. "You're alone."

"Quite," said Emma.

"Shall I have the fire lit?"

"No. I'm going out."

Tilda set the lamp on a table. "I'll help you dress." Once Emma had donned her purple overtunic, hose, and boots, Tilda reached for a comb. "Shall I plait your hair then?"

Emma hastened to the table and dropped onto the stool before it. "Aye," she said.

"One braid or two?"

"One. 'Tis faster."

Tilda combed Emma's thick, black tresses. "So," she said. "What happened last night?"

Emma sighed heavily.

"Not that I'm prying," Tilda continued. "I just...well, I worried about you all night."

"Thank you," said Emma, "but you needn't have. I said I'd refuse my husband, and I did."

The comb froze mid-stroke. "In the name of all that's holy, how did you survive to tell me about it?"

"We argued, and then he left."

"You spent the night alone?"

Emma slouched. "Entirely."

Tilda plunked the comb onto the table. Then, with speed and skill, she pulled and folded Emma's hair into a braid. "Where slept Lord Ravenwood?"

"Did he sleep?" Emma asked. "That's what I'd like to know."

"Did you?"

"Barely. And I've no idea where my husband spent the night."

Tilda cleared her throat. "I doubt he'll stay away forever, my lady."

Emma shivered. "I'm sure you're right."

"Then what can we do?"

"Hope. And pray."

"For what?"

"A miracle."

Tilda tied off the end of the braid, then attended to Emma's headrail. At last, she announced, "Done."

Emma sprang from the stool and grabbed her mantle. "Thank you, Tilda."

The handmaiden bit her lip. "Wither will you go?"

"Woden's Circle."

"Do you seek another vision?"

"No, but that's not a bad idea. Perhaps I could force the issue."

Tilda gave her a tentative smile. "Well, good luck."

"I could use some," Emma said. Then she hurried out the door.

She rushed down the spiral staircase and past the great hall, where some of the feast's more enthusiastic revelers snored with vigor. Descending the steps to the bailey, she avoided the many faces of Ravenwood, but she could feel their eyes on her. She understood their curiosity. They'd hardly be human if they didn't wonder about her first night with the new lord.

She exchanged glances with only one person, and that was Oswald, the stout, redheaded gateman. She gave him a brief smile, then scurried through the gatehouse, over the drawbridge, and out to the freedom beyond.

For the first time since exiting the keep, she looked skyward. A swarm of gray clouds cloaked the sun. The playful, yet insistent wind tugged at her mantle. She reveled in the fresh, crisp air and the liberty it represented. Whatever became of her marriage, her love of nature would endure.

She skipped across the fields and up the hill to Woden's Circle. Then she hesitated. Wulfstan leaned against one of the stones and gazed into the dark forest.

"Good morrow," she said.

Wulfstan turned. His furrowed brow smoothed, and he grinned.

"Good morrow," he replied. "I didn't expect to see you here."

"Nor I you." She entered the circle.

She chose the stone closest to the one he favored and leaned against it. 'Twas cold against her back, but firm and real.

"Of course, I'm not wholly surprised," Wulfstan said. "This was always one of your favorite places."

"And yours. Whenever you were close by."

He studied her face. "Sleepless night?"

She groaned. "'Tis that obvious?"

He nodded, and his light blue eyes seemed to radiate compassion.

"You've circles under your eyes too," she said. "Why?"

His frown returned. "All night, I've had the sense that something's wrong."

"Can you be more specific?"

He shook his head. "I would I could. The feeling is annoyingly vague."

"It may stem from Aldred's hasty departure."

He grinned. "That was rude, but I must say I'm the happier for it."

She returned his grin. "So am I."

"You were a beautiful bride, Emma."

"Thank you, but I trow you'd make an even better looking bridegroom."

He rolled his eyes. "Not if the gods are kind. My time is better spent learning the ancient arts."

She folded her arms. "And nothing else?"

He looked wistful. "Just think of me as a lone wolf, content to bay at the beauty and mystery of the moon."

"I think the wolf cries out to the moon because he's lonely."

"Not this wolf."

"Very well," she conceded. "Have your solitude, then."

"Are you here for a vision?"

"Not today."

"You sound disappointed."

Her arms dropped to her sides. "In a way, I am. Why can't I make it happen?"

"You know as well as I. We can focus our energy, even mold it to our will at times. But most often, the images come when they will. They flow to their own rhythm."

"You sound like Meg."

"I suppose I do." He leaned his head back against the stone. His blond hair shone despite the hidden sun. "You know, I've always envied you. Your visions of the future have helped a lot of people. Even Aldred."

She made a face. "Don't remind me. But why should you envy me? You need only touch someone to have a vision."

"But I see the past. How can you save a person from what's already hurt him?"

"You cannot. But knowing his pain, you can better help him in the present."

He smiled. "Now you sound like Meg."

"I guess she's affected us both. If only she could influence my husband. He's so demanding."

A gust of wind stirred Wulfstan's heavy, blue cloak, and his eyes searched hers. "Was he demanding last night?"

"Not exactly."

"Then you explained the curse."

"I started to."

"You must do more. Tell your husband everything you know of it. How it began, how it makes you feel. Tell him of your latest visions."

Emma pulled away from the stone at her back. "You know of them?"

"Meg told me."

"How can I tell Lord Ravenwood? He'll think I'm crazy. Or worse, a witch."

"You are, in a manner of speaking...or you could be. The root of the word 'witch' means to twist or to bend."

She snorted. "I doubt I could bend his viewpoint even an inch."

Wulfstan folded his arms, and the wind whipped his hair into a wild, golden mane. "He'll be like most Normans, and many Saxons, for that matter. They reject the old ways and the reality of magic. But they can't keep us from knowing the truth, any more than your husband can stop your speaking it."

"I don't know. Those who cannot see dismiss those who can."

"But you can make him see. The longer he knows you, and the more he experiences your world, the sooner he'll understand."

She stared into the shadows of the forest. "And if he doesn't?"

Wulfstan's expression was grave. "He will, Emma. He must."

****

William climbed the stairs to his bedchamber two at a time. The heavy door was ajar, revealing Tilda's plump form leaning over the empty bed. Oblivious to his presence, she smoothed out the rumpled sheets.

He pushed the door, and it yawned audibly. The handmaiden jumped.

"My lord!" she cried. Then she bobbed before him. "I didn't know...I didn't hear—"

"Obviously." He glanced about the chamber. "Where is your mistress?"

"Woden's Circle."

"Again?"

"Aye, my lord."

"Gave she any reason?"

"No, but I imagine she's restless."

Small wonder, he thought. He himself felt like a caged beast. After all, he'd spent his wedding night in a prison.

Perhaps a brisk walk was in order. A good stretch of the legs, at the end of which waited his reluctant bride.

"Was she alone?" he asked.

Tilda wrung her hands. "I trow so. 'Tis not unusual. 'Tis her favorite place."

"Mmm," William hummed.

The maidservant lowered her gaze to her twisting hands.

He looked sharply at her. "You seem nervous."

She looked up at him. "Aye, my lord."

"Do I scare you?"

"Aye, my lord."

His lips twitched. "Carry on," he said. Then he retraced his steps down the spiral stairs and headed for the bailey.

The wind that swept through the courtyard was cool and refreshing. Beyond the curtain wall, 'twas a strong, primal force. It snatched at his black mantle, teased his hair, and stung his cheeks. And it reminded him of Emma.

The true Emma, he mused. *The one hiding beneath the surface.*

He would uncover that side of her nature. One day, she herself would embrace it. That was the plan, at any rate.

He smiled into the wind. He'd had many a sorrier task.

The fertile soil of fields that were now his accommodated his steps, and the half-mile walk to Woden's Circle flew by. He tackled the final hill with long, powerful strides. Then he stopped short at the sound of voices.

"I'd better head back," Emma said. "Lord Ravenwood might be looking for me."

A low, male voice answered her. "And he wouldn't welcome finding us together."

She was with Wulfstan.

William frowned. Yet his steps were smooth and precise as he crested the hill and cut through the stone circle.

His voice sliced the wind. "You are both correct."

Standing but an arm's length apart, they turned to

him as one. Guilt haunted their faces.

Emma attempted a smile. "My lord," she said.

"My lady," he answered through his teeth.

Husband and wife glared at each other for a long, tense moment.

Wulfstan shifted his weight from one leg to the other. Then he broke the silence. "I'll take my leave now."

"Stay," William hissed. "There's no need to pretend anymore."

"We met by accident," Wulfstan said. "I was already here when she arrived."

"'Tis true," Emma said. "I swear it."

William's gaze slashed from one to the other, then settled on his wife. "Like you swore your empty vows in the chapel? You make a mockery of duty."

She lifted her chin and stabbed him with her cold, violet stare. "How dare you?"

"I dare because you've lied since the day we met," he retorted.

"No," she said. "You're lying to yourself!"

"Open your eyes, Norman," said Wulfstan. "We are but two old friends sharing memories."

"And a lover's tryst?" William pressed. His hand itched to grab his sword, but that wouldn't win him a place in Emma's bed. "I want the truth, Saxon."

Wulfstan's eyes were like crystal fire. "You've already heard it."

Emma approached William and touched his arm. Her hand was light, and her eyes were now soft. "Please believe us."

All of a sudden, William wanted to believe. He looked from Emma to Wulfstan, then back again.

"Perhaps I was mistaken," he grumbled.

Her relief was palpable. "Aye," she said. "You were."

Wulfstan took a step toward them. "If our places were reversed, I might've thought the same thing."

William regarded him in silence. He was in no mood for camaraderie.

Wulfstan glanced at the darkening sky. "Now I *shall* take my leave, before the rain washes me back to Ravenwood. I suggest you two hurry after."

"We'll be along shortly," said Emma. "I would speak with my husband."

Wulfstan gave her a meaningful look, then bowed to each of them in turn. "Emma. Lord Ravenwood." His royal blue mantle swirled to life as he turned and disappeared down the hill.

William turned to her. "Well?"

She stared at him. "I—" she began, but the forest interrupted her. A twig snapped. Wings fluttered.

She twisted around and peered into the trees. Then she looked back at him and shrugged. "One of the ravens, no doubt."

He nodded. "You were saying?"

"Right. There are things I must tell you."

"Things?"

"About the curse."

A second crack sounded from within the forest. Instinct warned William of danger before his mind could. There was a slight rustle, then a whoosh filled the air. He lunged in front of Emma to shield her.

As if time itself had slowed, a flurry of vivid thoughts seized his mind. He should've ridden Thunder, should've worn his chain mail. His wife was in peril.

They were both horribly exposed.

Then came searing pain as an arrow pierced his left arm. Emma screamed behind him. If he'd hesitated even a second, the arrow would've punctured her chest.

"Wulfstan!" she shouted.

Gritting his teeth, William grasped the back end of the arrow and snapped it off. He threw it to the ground and dashed toward the trees. Within the forest, a horse whinnied, then pounded its hooves into a gallop.

William clutched his injured bicep and warmth trickled over his fingers. "God's teeth!" he swore as the hoof beats receded in the distance.

He turned back to the circle, and a sharp pain lanced the length of his arm. Wincing, he looked down. There was more blood than he'd imagined.

Emma rushed toward him with Wulfstan close behind.

"Did you see anyone?" Wulfstan asked.

William shook his head, and the motion made him dizzy. "It sounded like one man," he said, panting. "We must find him."

"You're in no condition to look for anyone." Emma grabbed his good arm. "We must get you back to the keep and remove the arrow immediately."

"No," William argued. "The attacker may have left something behind that could lead us to him. I must search."

"Allow me," said Wulfstan. "That wound needs tending."

Wulfstan scrutinized the damaged arm. He reached toward the arrow's broken shaft, and William swatted his hand away. As their fingers touched, Wulfstan froze, and his eyes glazed over.

"Wulfstan?" said Emma.

He didn't budge or respond in any way.

She grabbed his shoulders and shook him. "Not now!"

Wulfstan flinched. Then he shook his head as if to clear it.

"You saw something," she said.

Wulfstan's face was pale and beaded with sweat. "I cannot discuss it."

"Cannot or will not?" she countered.

William had no idea what they were blathering about, or why the Saxon looked as though he'd seen a ghost. He only knew his arm was on fire.

Wulfstan turned to him. "Can you walk without help?"

"I've had far worse wounds," William said, but his vision had blurred. He was beginning to wonder if the arrow's tip was poisoned. "I'll notify my men at once. Robert will bring a search party to aid you."

Wulfstan nodded. "I could also use my horse."

"Done," said William.

Wulfstan turned to Emma. "Get your husband back to the keep."

Emma gave him a pointed look. "But later, I'll have your answer."

Wulfstan avoided her gaze. He hurried into the Long Wood and dissolved like a wraith into its shadows.

William had no choice but to let Wulfstan look where he could not. His arm burned, and his head swam. Yet someone had to search while the trail was fresh. The clouds above were heavy, threatening. A few minutes more, and the rain might wash away any clues that remained.

If Wulfstan didn't steal them first.

William blinked. Shadows crept into his line of vision. They grew larger and more intrusive by the second. Even so, he spied a conspiracy of ravens perched atop one of the ancient stones. They watched him...and waited.

Emma's arm slipped around his waist. "Come," she said. "Let's get you home."

"Home," he repeated.

'Twas a pleasant word. Almost a prayer. And 'twas his last thought before the world went black.

Chapter Ten

The rain pummeled the keep and drowned the midnight moon. Emma stared down at her husband's sleeping form. 'Twas his first slumber in their bedchamber, in a bed she'd never shared. And because she'd spent most of the afternoon and evening tending his wound, this moment provided her first chance to admire his bare chest.

She'd healed men of all shapes and sizes, but this Norman was quite the specimen. His muscles were well-defined. His skin was like fine linen, shiny and smooth, yet covered with dark, curly hair and the scars of a warrior.

Her shock over the attack had doubled once she realized the arrow was poisoned. The sight of William lying helpless on the ground was frightening, unthinkable. Somehow she hadn't thought of him as mortal.

She did now. If her knowledge of herbs had been any less, or if Robert hadn't already been riding toward Woden's Circle, William would've died.

There was still danger. His skin burned, and his head tossed on the pillow as fever gripped his dreams. Intermittently, he mumbled a strange language.

She bit her lower lip. *If only I could heal his nightmares,* she thought.

He moaned and gripped the sheet covering his

waist. "Sahar," he whispered.

She recognized the word, though its meaning was unclear. He'd said it over and over.

Three loud thumps sounded on the chamber door, and she started. She hurried to the door and poised her hands over the bolt.

"Who's there?" she called.

"Sir Robert," was the muffled reply.

With a sigh, she unbolted the door. Then she swung it open.

Robert's gray eyes took in the scene at a glance. "You're still dressed," he said.

"I don't expect to sleep," she answered. "Do come in."

He crossed the threshold. With hands clasped behind his back, he advanced toward the bed.

She closed the door and turned back to Robert. He stared down at his brother for a long moment. Then he moved to the fireplace and frowned at the blaze within.

She hastened toward the hearth. "Please," she said, gesturing to the high-backed chair before the fire. "Sit."

Robert dropped onto the chair, and she pulled up a stool to join him.

"Thank you for tending William," he said.

"He is my husband."

He gave her a searching look. "So you don't want to be rid of him."

"Of course not."

"I'm glad to hear it."

"Your brother deserves the best care I can give him. 'Tis for my sake he lies wounded."

"What?"

"I've told no one, but the arrow was meant for

me."

"Then William jumped in front of you."

"Without a thought for himself."

"That sounds like my brother."

"And I'm in his debt."

Firelight skipped and swayed in Robert's eyes. "How very odd," he said. "'Tis Norman blood that's prized in these hills."

Emma shuddered despite the roaring fire. "I know, but the intent was clear. The attacker wanted me dead."

"All the more reason to discover his identity."

She nodded. "Gertrude heard Aldred's men talking before they left. Apparently, there's a band of ruffians in the area."

"Robbers?"

"'Tis rumored so."

"But why would you be a target?"

"Why not?"

"No," he said, rubbing his chin. "There's more to this."

She studied his face. 'Twas so like William's. Intelligent, hard, yet kinder somehow. "I was told that Wulfstan found nothing," she said.

"That's right."

"I wish I'd had a chance to speak with him."

"Aye. 'Tis remarkable how fast he flew north after finding 'nothing.'"

"Wulfstan isn't to blame for any of this."

"You're quick to defend him."

"I'd defend anyone falsely accused."

Robert grunted. "We shall see."

"Yes," she said pointedly. "You shall."

He grinned. "It must be your stubbornness that

makes you such a gifted healer."

"Meg's far more talented. Wulfstan has a knack for healing too."

"I'm sure William prefers your ministrations," he said wryly. He glanced toward the bed where William still moaned in his sleep, and his smile disappeared. "He will come out of it, won't he?"

She refused to voice her fears. "I believe so," she said. "A weaker man might not have survived. But the wound is clean, and my medicines appear to be working. If he makes it through the night, he should recover within days."

"I hope you're right."

I have to be, she thought. *William saved my life, and I can do no less for him.*

Robert was watching her again. "You'll not find a stronger man than William," he said, as if to reassure her.

"I believe you," she said.

"He's faced horrors you cannot imagine."

Her gaze drifted to the bed. "Do you think he dreams of them now?"

His expression grim, Robert nodded. She could almost feel his sorrow reaching out to her. Perhaps, out of habit, he kept the emotion locked away, and 'twas all the stronger for it.

"Of what horrors do you speak?" she asked.

"Besides the endless engine of war and death to which a knight is privy?"

"Aye."

"Try torture."

Her mouth went dry. "What?" she croaked.

Robert glared at the fire. "Surely you've noticed

William's hands. How both little fingers are misshapen, with each knuckle twisted."

"I've seen plenty of broken bones," she said. "I assumed his hadn't been set properly."

"That much is true, but the bones were broken deliberately."

She gasped. "For what? Information?"

"For pleasure. And that was a mere prelude to other, more imaginative torments."

Heat flooded her cheeks. "Who would do such a thing?"

As if he would answer through his delirium, William mumbled from the bed.

"Do you know what he's speaking?" Robert asked.

"No."

"Turkish, one of the Saracen tongues. The language of William's torturer."

"Who was he?"

"A rich and powerful chief known as Hattin the Horrid. He had many wives and even more lemans. His favorite leman was Sahar."

"So that's what he's been saying! A name."

"One he'll never forget," said Robert. "Sahar was renowned for her beauty. Dark hair, dark eyes, and skin the color of bronze. She escaped Hattin's fortress and found her way to our encampment. Her tales of abuse angered William, and he offered her his protection. With time, affection grew between them. I think William came as close to loving Sahar as he could any woman."

"Truly?"

Robert nodded. "But she'd caught another man's eye, and he betrayed them. William was captured and thrown into the pit of hell, a torture chamber devised and lovingly operated by Hattin himself."

"What happened to Sahar?"

"She seemed to disappear from the face of the earth."

"And the man who betrayed them?"

"We never learned his identity."

"But someone must've seen or heard something."

"Sadly not. William was alone when it happened. He'd been lured to a spot far from camp where Sahar supposedly awaited him. Later, when William's men learned of his imprisonment, they were more concerned with freeing him than seeking vengeance."

"Was there a ransom?"

"We tried that road first, but every time we arrived with a payment, Hattin raised the ransom. It became clear he had no interest in gold, only William's pain."

"For what reason? Revenge?"

"That, and a place in legend as the man who humbled William the Storm."

Bile rose in her throat. "The man was a beast!"

"No argument here," said Robert. "In the end, we besieged Hattin's fortress and rescued William."

She shook her head. "I had no idea."

"How could you? I've often wished I didn't, but there's no avoiding my brother's moods."

"I'm well aware of them."

"He was never quite the same after his capture."

"I can understand why."

"I was hoping you would."

She peered into the depths of his eyes. "Thank you for telling me."

He stood. "You earned it, through your actions

today."

She walked him to the door. "Sleep well tonight. I'll watch over Lord Ravenwood."

Warmth—and perhaps newfound trust—softened Robert's features. "I know you will." He started down the stairs.

Emma closed the door and returned to William. With care, she stretched out on the bed beside him. Maybe a part of him would sense her presence, and 'twould comfort him.

She frowned. His body heat seemed every bit as strong as the flames in the hearth.

The fever must break soon, she thought.

Until it did, she could only wait.

She bit her lip and ran her fingers through his chest hair. 'Twas soft and springy. She stretched out her palm and held it just above his chest, then slowly moved her hand from one side to the other. The hair tickled her palm.

"Sahar," William murmured.

He was dreaming of her. His Saracen temptress. His beloved. Had Sahar touched him in the same way she did now?

Emma pursed her lips. Why should she care if he'd loved before? Her goal was to keep him out of her bed...and guard her life.

But William had already saved it. Without regard for himself, he'd leapt in front of her and intercepted the poisoned arrow. Why?

The shutters at the window shook from the force of the wind outside. Unending rain lashed its fury on wood and stone.

"Sahar," William said again.

She soothed his fevered brow, then leaned forward. "No," she whispered in his ear. "Emma."

****

William woke to the high, whistling melody of a bird perched on the windowsill. If the idea weren't absurd, he might sing himself. 'Twas the first time in three days he'd opened his eyes without triggering an intense headache. His vision had cleared, and the hole in his arm had lost its sting. 'Twas still sore, but that was to be expected.

Experimentally, he pushed himself into a sitting position. Most of his strength had returned, and he felt remarkably well. 'Twas either a miracle or the result of Emma's excellent care. Perhaps a bit of both.

From the moment he'd first regained consciousness, he knew she was there. She hadn't said much over the last few days, but she'd tended his wound, seen to his comfort, and slept on a pallet beside the bed. She'd seemed determined to ease his pain, to pass on her strength to him. Through the blur of fatigue and confusion, he'd been grateful.

But where was she now? Her sleeping pallet was gone, and the door was unbolted. The shutters were open to a bright, crisp day.

A sudden echo of footsteps and conversation rose from the stairwell and grew nearer by the second. He strained to hear and recognized the voices. 'Twas a golden opportunity, and he had to take advantage of it. Rearranging the bedclothes, he lay back down and feigned sleep.

The door creaked. Then the floor rushes crunched as the women entered the chamber.

"I still don't understand," Gertrude whispered.

"Why didn't you just let him die?"

"He's my husband," Emma said.

"All of your problems would've been solved," Gertrude persisted. "Instead, you fawn over him and dig yourself into a deeper hole."

"I'm in no hole."

"Aren't you? You'd better think again, Emma. And caring for his men is just as bad. Why trouble yourself over the aches and pains of Norman murderers?"

"'Tis what I do, and I'll continue to help others whether they be Saxons, Normans, or the ghost of William the Conqueror himself."

"Even you cannot heal the dead."

"Then I suggest you leave, before my husband hears your insults and kills you."

William struggled to keep his mouth slack. Emma had spine; that was certain.

One of the women—presumably Gertrude—stomped across the floor. The door banged shut. Then a rustle of footsteps approached the bed.

The mattress shifted as Emma sat beside him. Her scent was sweet, familiar. Intoxicating. He felt her gaze on him, so he lay still and measured each breath.

Suddenly, her soft, cool hand found his chest. 'Twas a tentative touch, and a telling one.

Aye, he thought. *Feel me, Wife. Know me. I'm not your enemy.*

She slid her fingers through his chest hair and over his ribs. Then, with one finger, she circled a nipple. The flesh hardened in response.

Control, he thought. *I must keep control.*

Her hand was now warm. It had sucked up his body heat as a flower drank from the sun. Her fingers traced his scars, and he remembered their infliction; the how, where, and why of every wound. If Emma's bane was the Ravenwood curse, his was a perfect memory.

Abruptly, her actions pulled him back to the present. Her hand slipped lower, down his torso. She tugged at the hair on his belly and poked a playful finger into his navel.

His entire body hardened. If she shoved the fur coverlet just two inches lower, his arousal would be plain.

He opened his eyes. "Does my flesh please you?"

She yanked her hand from his stomach. "No," she said. "I mean, aye."

He grinned. "I'm glad to hear it."

Her cheeks were beet red. "I meant no disrespect. I thought you were sleeping, and I was…curious."

"Well, I'm not stopping you. You've a healing touch. Continue."

"I'd rather not."

"Wouldn't you?"

"'Twas brazen of me."

"But not unwelcome."

Her eyes narrowed. "I shall feed you instead."

He smiled wickedly. "I've a much longer fast to break."

The color drained from her face. "That may be, but I've your health to consider."

His hand found her thigh. "What could be healthier?"

"Medicine for your wound. I'll fetch it from my workshop."

She scooted off of the bed, but he grabbed her arm. "No," he said. "Stay with me."

She hesitated, and her brow crinkled as she stared down at him. In the sunlight, her skin was luminous as a pearl, and her eyes glittered in the softest shade of purple. She'd never looked lovelier.

Slowly, she sat back down. "I'll stay, but only for a little while. And only because I want to."

He smiled. "You have spirit enough to intoxicate a legion of warriors."

"I have no desire to intoxicate anyone."

"Too late."

Her gaze dropped to her pink tunic. She cleared her throat, then looked up at him again. "You seem greatly improved this morning."

"I am, because of you."

"'Tis I who should be grateful. The venomous arrow should've struck me."

"Then 'twas poisoned. Just as I thought. Did my men find anything?"

"No."

"Did Wulfstan?"

"No again, and he left that afternoon."

"Hmm."

She cleared her throat. "We've done our best to make you comfortable."

"We?"

"I see you've little memory of the past three days. Meg and Tilda helped me care for you. Your brother looked in on you, too. Everyone's been concerned."

"Everyone?"

"Well, not Gertrude."

"And you?"

"I've devoted myself to your recovery. That speaks for itself."

His gaze dropped to her exquisite hands. "Tell me, why were you so curious about my body this morning? Didn't you bathe me while I was ill?"

"Meg did."

He frowned. "Did my scarred flesh disgust you? I'm sure many a maid would snivel or shriek at the sight of it."

Her eyes flared. "I'm no shallow, lily-livered maid to judge a person by his skin. What do you take me for?"

"I'm not sure. I'm still trying to work out why you won't take me."

She sobered. "I was hoping you'd forgiven me by now. Our wedding night was not one of my better moments."

He grunted. "Nor one of mine."

"Yet despite my behavior, you saved my life."

"Aye."

"Why did you?"

He didn't know how to answer her. It had been instinct, an inexplicable need to shield her from harm. "I protect what is mine," he said gruffly.

She slid off the bed and backed away. "I see," she said, her voice flat. "'Tis an honor to be so highly prized."

With a stiff gait, she walked to the door. Then she paused.

"You're obviously well enough to break your own fast," she said, still facing the door. "I'll send Tilda up with medicine and fresh bandages. She knows what to do."

William sat up and swung his legs over the edge of the bed. "Emma," he said.

"Good morrow," she replied as she left the room. Her footfalls patted down the staircase until they disappeared altogether.

Chapter Eleven

High on Ravenwood's stone walls, the castle bees were hard at work inside their straw skeps. Emma stared at the row of hives and willed herself to think of something other than William. It had been hours since the scene in the bedchamber, and like the bees buzzing in front of her, she'd busied herself with daily tasks. She had to keep moving and keep unwanted thoughts at bay.

She'd climbed to this lofty corner of the keep with a fresh supply of hound's-tongue lotion for the beekeeper, but the man was nowhere to be seen. Since she hated to leave any errand half-done, she waited for him.

Barely a minute passed before inevitable reflection crept in.

I protect what is mine, William's voice echoed in her mind.

He thought of her as a possession, like jewels, arms, land, and any other object he could own and control. She'd known that from the beginning. 'Twas ridiculous that it bothered her now. Yet it did.

"My lady," said a voice beside her.

Emma snapped out of her reverie and focused her attention on Roderic, the beekeeper. The thick netting attached to the elderly man's hat obscured his face, but his gentle voice and hunched shoulders were unmistakable. And like a fully armed knight, a beekeeper's costume left no doubt as to his profession.

"Forgive me for startling you," Roderic said.

She flashed him a smile as warm as the sun above. "I'm glad you did," she said. "I brought you more lotion."

She held out the bottle to him, and he removed one of his heavy gloves to take it. He dropped it into the pouch at his waist and gave it a gentle pat.

"Thank you," he said. "Nothing soothes a bee sting better than one of your ointments."

"As your assistant well knows," she said with a wink. While Roderic could charm bees, his assistant seemed to enrage them.

Roderic squinted at the sky, and she followed his gaze. White clouds that resembled fat, wooly sheep dotted the field of blue.

"Our weather is much improved, now that Wulfstan is gone," the beekeeper said.

She scanned the clouds, for what she didn't know. Perhaps a clue to Wulfstan's vision the day of the attack. What had he seen? What was he hiding?

"My lady," said Roderic, "what troubles you?"

"Not a thing," she said, avoiding his gaze. "I'm perfectly well, but I must get back to work. Let me know when you need more lotion."

She hurried back to her workshop. Tilda was waiting there with her little brother, Martin. Another redhead with big brown eyes, Martin had turned five the month before. He ran forward and hugged Emma's legs.

"Oh, Martin!" Tilda scolded.

Emma laughed and bent down to him. "What a

116

wonderful surprise! How's your arm?"

"Good as new." Martin held out the tiny limb as proof.

Emma examined it and smiled.

Tilda nodded. "That's why we're here, to thank you again for mending it," she said. Then she gave her brother a sideways look. "Though there would've been no need if he hadn't fancied himself a knight and leapt off that haystack."

"I had to fight the Saracens," Martin explained.

"They were pigs, as I remember it," Tilda said.

"Not to me," Martin protested.

Tilda sighed, then tweaked his cherubic cheeks. "Little devil," she said.

Suddenly, William blocked the doorway and all sunlight beyond. "If you're speaking of devils, why not let another one join you?" he said affably. "May I?"

His eyes glittered with charm and a hint of mischief. Clothed in black and unnervingly tall now that he was back on his feet, he might well have been Lucifer himself.

Emma straightened as he entered the workshop. "My medicine must be powerful indeed."

"'Twas applied most skillfully," he said, and his gaze shifted from Emma to her handmaiden. "Wasn't it, Tilda?"

Tilda gulped. "If you say so, my lord."

William regarded the boy at her hip. "And who is this?"

"Martin," said Tilda.

"Her brother," Emma added.

"Ah," said William. "Martin, why have you come to Lady Ravenwood's workshop?"

"To thank her for fixing my arm," the boy said. "I broke it."

"How?" William asked.

"I was fighting Saracens," Martin said.

"Pigs," Tilda amended.

With a chortle, William knelt before Martin. "I understand," he said, as though they were two warriors sharing a confidence. "Saracens may be the enemy, but we must admit they're clever and strong."

"And brave?" said Martin.

William grinned. "Very, just like you."

Martin's freckled nose crinkled as he smiled. His eyes shone with adoration for the knight who'd bestowed the highest praise of his young life.

William stood and ruffled the boy's fiery hair. "Fight the next battle for me, lad."

"I will," Martin promised.

Emma was speechless. William l'Orage was a proud man. A feared one. He'd suffered unnamable tortures, yet his heart was agile enough to treat a child with kindness.

Tilda's eyes were wide and focused on William. "We'll be going now." She grabbed her brother's hand.

Martin broke away and hugged Emma once more. Her heart swelled with affection, and she kissed his cheek.

"Thank you for coming," she said.

Tilda ushered Martin through the open door. Hand in hand, they skipped off into the herb garden.

"He's a fine boy," William said.

Emma turned to William and spied a look of longing on his face. It vanished quickly, but it had been there. She took a step closer to him.

"I know why Martin was here," she said. "Why are you?"

He grinned at her. "I've come to offer a truce."

She raised her eyebrows. "Really," she said, unable to mask the skepticism in her voice. "What are the terms?"

"We put aside our differences and learn about each other. After all, we'll be together a long time."

Only if I can keep you out of my bed, she thought, but she answered, "I accept."

"Good," he said. "We'll start now, unless you have more pressing affairs."

"I'd planned to check my inventory, but that can wait. What shall we do?"

"What would you suggest?"

She considered the options. "I'd love to go hunting."

"So would I, but 'twould be ill-advised so soon after the attack. We should stay close to the keep."

"How about Woden's Circle?"

"'Tis still your favorite place?"

"One bad event cannot destroy a lifetime of memories."

He regarded her for a long moment, then nodded. "Very well. But I insist that some of my men accompany us."

"Will we have any privacy?" she asked.

His black eyes seemed to glow. "How much do you require?"

"Enough to speak without being overheard."

"That much? I'm pleased you want to be alone with me."

Sweat beaded on her forehead and upper lip. "You

mistake my meaning. Our conversation could easily become fodder for idle tongues, and I'd rather it didn't."

"You have a point. I'll post my men close enough to guard us, but out of hearing range. Will that suit you?"

"Aye. One question, though. Will Geoffrey be in the party?"

"My squire? Probably. Why?"

"I promised him some monk's-hood oil."

"Monk's-hood?"

"'Tis also known as wolfsbane. It makes a soothing rub for aching joints."

"Does Geoffrey ache?"

"He has ever since Guy bested him at swordplay yesterday."

"Ah. Those two are good friends and even better competitors. Since there's no tonic for a bruised ego, you'd better bring the oil."

She grabbed a small bottle from the shelf behind him. "Got it," she said.

He smiled and offered her his good arm. "Then let's go."

****

High atop Thunder, William glanced at the approaching clouds on the horizon. The cool wind rippled through his hair like a benediction. He lowered his gaze to drink in the sight of Emma on her mount up ahead. Watching her ride the brown jennet to Woden's Circle was worth the whole outing. Her grace and posture befitted a queen. If King Henry's bards had tagged along, they would've gained ripe material for poetic verse from her easy movements in the saddle.

Her veil billowed behind her, offering a tantalizing glimpse of her raven hair beneath.

Robert, Geoffrey, Guy, and five other battle-hardened men completed the party. When they reached the circle, William deployed the men for their watch, then followed Emma into the pagan site.

She leaned back against one side of the central stone piling. "I feel better already," she said, smiling.

So did he. He breathed deeply of the scent of pine needles, then exhaled slowly. All at once, his wound began to tingle. He raised his opposite hand and touched the tight bandage beneath his tunic.

"'Tis working," Emma said.

"What?" he asked.

"The magic of Woden's Circle. Something about this place speeds the healing process. I've experienced it myself."

"I don't believe in magic."

"Apparently, it believes in you." She pointed to his arm.

He shook his head. "Ridiculous."

"Say what you will, but magic exists. 'Tis a force as natural as the wind, and we are all a part of it. Some people just sense it more than others."

"Are you telling me you're one of those people?"

"I am. I wanted to tell you the other day, but the attack interfered."

He regarded her in silence. "Go on," he said at last.

She fiddled with her long, pink sleeves. Then she stilled. "From an early age, I had visions of the future. Sometimes they were clear and sometimes not, but always they warned me of danger."

"Danger to you?"

"And to others."

"I assume you had no warning of the arrow attack."

"I wish I had. I don't plan the visions. I just know when they're about to happen. I get an irresistible urge to come hither, and the circle's energy helps me focus. That's why you found me here the day we met."

"You sought a vision?"

"I did."

"I see. The energy you mentioned, is that why you love it here?"

"'Tis one reason, but its haunting beauty draws me even more. Sometimes, when I'm standing alone in the mist, I almost believe my ancestors will step from behind the stones."

"What would you say to them if they did?"

She smiled. "I'd welcome them and learn more about their beliefs and daily lives."

"And their language?"

"Aye. That, too."

"I begin to understand your attraction to this place."

"Do languages interest you?"

"Like mother's milk interests a newborn."

Without warning, sorrow swept over her features.

"Does that bother you?" he asked.

"No," she said, her eyes downcast. "I was thinking of my mother. I feel closer to her here."

"'Tis said she died at your birth."

Emma nodded. "Courtesy of the Ravenwood curse."

William shifted from one foot to the other. Visions were unlikely, but curses were impossible. Yet she believed it all, and he would hear her out.

"Tell me about the curse," he said. "Do you know how it began?"

"The first Lord Ravenwood lived here more than two centuries ago," Emma said. "He followed the old religion, and 'tis said he worked magic as deftly as a tailor wields needle and thread. He loved his wife passionately, but she had a roving eye. She betrayed him with another man, and he flew into a rage. Then he learned she was pregnant. She swore the child was his, but his doubt drove him mad. He cursed our line, deeming that every Lady Ravenwood would die in childbirth, unless the child was conceived through true love."

He scratched his head. "But why?" he asked. "It seems foolish to make love a condition when most marriages are arranged."

"I know, but he wanted to protect future lords of Ravenwood, especially those who would love their wives as he loved his. If lust tempted the women and they conceived a child, they'd die."

"What if love tempted them?"

"It never happened. And apparently, none of Ravenwood's ladies loved their husbands, because every one of them died in childbirth."

"Every one?"

"'Tis true. Daughters of Ravenwood live and perish under the curse. The only boon is that we're born with magical talents. We're gifted healers, and many have the Sight."

"Have there been no sons born to Ravenwood?"

"A few, but when they married, the curse claimed their wives as well."

William ran his hand over the cold, rough surface

of the nearest stone. "So wedded bliss is as scarce at Ravenwood as everywhere else," he said. "But a curse? That I cannot believe."

"Do you think it natural for all of those women to die in childbirth?"

"It happens."

"Not on that scale, in one place."

"Coincidence."

"No, William. 'Tis real."

He warmed to the sound of his name on her tongue. "How can you be certain?"

She stared into the forest behind him. Then she pushed her shoulders back and regarded him once more. "I've had repeated visions of my mother warning me of danger."

"How did she warn you?"

"She showed me an image of myself lying pale and still as death."

A chill coursed the length of his spine, but he shook it off. "Perhaps your visions warned of the recent attack. If you'd been alone, you would've died."

She tilted her head in the familiar movement which made her look like a raven pondering flight. "I hadn't thought of that," she said. "I haven't had the vision since the attack, so maybe you're right."

An unexpected need seized him. He had to give her hope.

"I know I'm right," he said. "And I will always protect you."

She favored him with a tentative, tender smile. "Thank you."

He shook his head. "Thank *you* for sharing your burden with me."

She stared at him for a long moment, then folded her arms. "Enough about me," she said. "Let's talk about you."

"There's little to say."

She raised her eyebrows. "I doubt that."

He showed her a mock frown. "We're married less than a week, and already you doubt my word."

"Not your word. Your modesty."

He shrugged. "I'm not modest, just reluctant to speak."

"An odd trait for a man who loves languages."

He took a step closer to her. "You are the most vexing woman."

She grinned. "Stubborn too."

He sighed. "You may ask questions. But for every one I answer, I shall ask one of you."

"Fair enough," she said. "First question: were you an unruly child?"

"Very. Were you?"

"No, but I still irritated my father. He avoided me whenever possible and actually preferred Gertrude's company."

"Gertrude?" he said, his eyes wide. "'Tis hard to imagine."

Emma nodded. "Isn't it, though?"

"Scary, in fact."

She tilted her head. "I thought nothing scared you."

"I'll make an exception in Gertrude's case."

Emma laughed. "Right. Second question: how old were you when you became a knight?"

"Sixteen." He advanced another step. "My turn. Was I the first man to kiss you?"

Her cheeks flooded with the rosy shade of her

tunic. Backed against the tall stone, her violet eyes wide with surprise, she looked shockingly beautiful.

"What kind of question is that?" she asked.

"A simple one. I answered my question. Now you must."

She pursed her lips, and they riveted him. "You were the first."

Satisfaction, wanton and warm, flowed through him. "I'm glad of it."

"What's your favorite place?" she said quickly.

"Between a woman's thighs. And yours?"

Sweat glistened on her forehead and above her upper lip. 'Twould taste salty, yet sweet.

"Besides Woden's Circle?" she said.

"Aye."

"I guess the Long Wood."

He gave her a wolfish grin. "Some woods are longer than others."

Emotion flashed in her eyes. Then her expression turned droll. "Aye," she said. "I've noticed that horses are particularly well endowed."

He burst out laughing. "What a weapon your tongue would make."

"On the battlefield?"

"Or in bed, if you so desired."

She shook her head. "You think I'm vexing? The honor is yours, Lord Ravenwood."

"So formal. What happened to 'William?'"

"He traveled beyond the bounds of decency."

"Can he be saved?"

Her eyes twinkled. "Mayhap, if he limits his travels and stays closer to home."

"What if you could travel with him? Would that

please you?"

"Aye, so long as the pace was sufficiently slow."

He inched toward her. This was one double-edged meaning of which she was unaware, but he was not. "Quick or slow, my pace shall be as you command it."

"I'm not sure I understand," she said.

"You will. I promise."

He leaned forward to kiss her, and a cold raindrop splashed onto his nose. Another grazed his cheek, but his intent was firm. At the last second, she turned her mouth away, and his lips brushed her cheek instead.

"Oh," she said, raising her palm to the sky. She slid away from the stone and out of kissing range. "Rain. We should get back."

He grumbled. Maybe there was truth to her claims about Woden's Circle. She believed it enhanced her visions. Perhaps it protected her from the poisoned arrow. Did it shield her now from his kiss, through the guise of rain?

No, he thought. *Impossible.*

A sudden torrent of water besieged them.

"Blessed Virgin!" Emma cried. "You'd think the heavens opened up for the sole purpose of drenching us."

"Mount your horse," William said. "I'll signal to my men."

He turned his head to hide his smile. If magic did exist, it aided him too. There was only one thing to do with wet clothes: remove them.

Chapter Twelve

Emma shivered as she and William followed the cold, winding stairs to their bedchamber. Her clothes were soaked, and her husband's straight, white teeth were more visible than ever before. He just kept smiling, and his apparent glee unnerved her. There had to be a reason for it. God only knew what!

As they entered the chamber, her gaze darted from the closed shutters to the cold, empty hearth. There'd been no need for a fire before the storm; now, it seemed a neccssity. An oil lamp on the table was the only source of heat and light in the room.

She pivoted on her heel just as William slid the door's thick bolt into place. He turned to her and flashed yet another smile. Then he advanced with a slow, casual stride.

An aura of strength and sensuality shadowed his every move and trailed in his wake. The closer he came, the drier her mouth seemed. He halted scarcely a foot away.

She licked her lips. "Shall I have a servant light the fire?"

He stared down at her with black, hungry eyes. "There's no need. There are better ways to keep warm."

"But our clothes." She gestured to the garments which clung to her body. "They're drenched."

His eyes narrowed. "Surely you don't intend to

keep them on."

"The idea had occurred to me."

"Ridiculous. You look as uncomfortable as a wet cat."

"Comfort is highly overrated."

"Emma," he said in the tone of command he used with his men. "Your clothes are coming off. If not by your hand, by mine."

She hugged her torso and stepped backward. "How can you ask this of me? After all I've told you?"

He raised an eyebrow. "Is it wrong to prevent my wife from freezing to death?"

Her teeth chattered. "N-no, but I know where things can lead."

He rolled his eyes. "Your teeth sound like a jester's rattle. Do as I say."

He's right, she thought. If she didn't doff her wet garments soon, she'd be too sick to heal anyone else.

"You win," she said.

His teeth gleamed. "Do you need any help?"

She gave him a pointed look. "I can manage alone."

She removed her headdress, then lowered her gaze to her overtunic. The cloth was a darker shade of pink when wet, and heavier, too. Grumbling, she pulled it over her head and struggled out of it. When she emerged, she glanced at William. He hadn't budged.

"Well?" she said. "Are you just going to stand there leering at me?"

"The thought does appeal."

"Not to me."

"'Tis my right to watch."

"And mine to undress in peace. Now, go on.

You've wet clothes of your own to remove."

She turned her back and shuffled to the far wall, into which a row of wooden pegs was set. She hung her overtunic to dry, and a few squirms later, she placed her inner tunic beside it. Then she kicked aside her boots and peeled off her stockings.

All that remained was her white linen smock. 'Twas ankle length with a round neck and long, tightly-fitted sleeves. She ran her hands over the smooth cloth, then sighed with relief. The smock was mostly dry, and it covered enough of her body to offer a measure of protection. Safety was an illusion, but any fantasy helped.

She turned around, and her stomach dropped. William stood in the middle of the chamber wearing nothing but his braies. The loose linen covered him from hips to calves, but barely concealed the sculpted thighs within.

His gaze raked her from head to toe, and he smiled. "Just imagine," he said, "all that rain, and my breeches are dry."

Her gaze strayed to his muscular torso. "So is my smock," she said in a voice not quite her own.

He tugged on the string at his waist. "Still, I think I'll take them off."

"No! I mean, don't trouble yourself."

"'Tis no trouble, but in deference to your request, I'll leave them on."

She let out a long breath. "Thank you."

He bowed to her, and his wet hair shone like black damask. "My lady."

She tore her gaze away and pulled her long, thick braid over her shoulder. With extreme focus, she unraveled the plait, hoping to erase the image of William's godlike physique from her mind.

A telltale crackle of rushes warned of his approach. He stole past her and grabbed something from the nearby table. She looked up as he returned with a stool in one hand and her comb in the other.

He set down the stool and motioned to it. "Allow me," he said.

She hesitated. Then she shrugged and sat down. The cold from the wooden stool traveled easily through her thin smock to her backside, and she shuddered. The next instant, William stood close behind her. Heat, both welcome and disturbing, emanated from his body. He loosened the rest of her braid. Then he began to comb her hair with soothing, rhythmic strokes.

Slowly, she began to relax. The comb's movements were soft as a caress, and she hummed with pleasure before she could stop herself.

"This pleases you," he remarked. His voice was deep and rich, in perfect harmony with the lilting comb.

"Aye," she said. "If I were a cat, I'd purr."

"If you were a cat, your raven friends wouldn't come near you."

"True."

"But I would."

"As cat or man?"

The comb's strokes ceased. "Which answer will earn me another kiss?"

He knelt at her feet. He gazed up at her with a raven's dark, unfathomable eyes. His hands cupped her knees, infusing her with warmth through the thin linen barrier. Languidly, he slid his palms up her thighs.

She stiffened, and he stopped. His hands were so

large they stretched across the top half of her thighs. He bent lower and laid his head in her lap.

"Your chemise is soft," he murmured, "but I'll warrant your skin is softer."

She swallowed the lump in her throat. "You think so?"

He dropped his hands to her feet. "There's only one way to find out," he said. His fingers blazed a path from her ankles to her calves, where he squeezed the tender flesh. "I was right."

"William, I don't—"

"Just think of me as that tiny spaniel in the kennel," he cooed. Through the linen, he nuzzled her tightly clamped thighs.

"Tiny you are not."

"How would you know?" His hands now covered her bare knees.

She summoned her strength and pushed his hands aside. Hastily, she stood and backed away until her buttocks collided with the edge of the bed. "You know you cannot bed me."

In three strides, he crossed the distance between them. Mischief sparkled in his eyes. "There are other things we can do," he said.

Her mouth fell open. "What do you mean?"

He raised her hand to his lips. "Lovemaking has endless variations." He turned her palm upward and planted a kiss at its center.

She shivered. Perhaps there was a way to enjoy his attentions, yet keep her maidenhead intact. "Which variation do you have in mind?"

His arms encircled her. "I'd better show you," he whispered, and he lowered his mouth to hers.

His tongue traced her lower lip, then slipped inside her mouth. Her tongue caressed his. She raised her hands to his smooth, wet hair and slid her fingers through it. Instinctively, she pressed her hips against him...and felt a rock-hard bulge at her belly. With a gasp, she wriggled away.

He chuckled. "It won't bite. I promise."

"'Twas just...a surprise."

"There are more where that came from."

He cupped her buttocks and pulled her against him. Again, his arousal warmed her belly. His mouth reclaimed hers in a deep, passionate kiss. She was falling, deliciously dizzy, sucked into a maelstrom. She gave herself to the sensation and moaned with pleasure.

His moan echoed hers. He raised a hand to her left breast. Through the linen veil, his finger circled the nipple in the same rhythm as his tongue in her mouth.

Her pap hardened. Gently, he teased it, and his touch grew increasingly softer. With a groan, she bit his lower lip. Then she flattened his hand on her breast.

"My wild raven," he murmured.

He left a trail of kisses down her neck and chest as his lips moved lower and finally closed around the taut nipple. He sucked it, and his tongue lashed the tender flesh through her smock.

Her legs felt weak. She swayed and grabbed his shoulders.

"Aye," he said. "Hold tight."

He sucked her other teat and simultaneously reached beneath her smock. With a stealthy, light touch, his hand crept up her legs to the soft mound between them. He petted the hidden hair with the same smooth rhythm he'd created with the comb.

Her breath caught in her throat. She felt hypersensitive, expectant. All she could do was close her eyes and surrender to his feather-light strokes.

He knelt and kissed her belly through the smock. Beneath the garment, his caress slowed. He parted her damp curls and ran a single finger along the tiny, hot crevice, from its apex to the wider, wet opening.

"Emma," he breathed. "A man would kill to be inside you."

All at once, his finger slipped an inch into her.

She gasped and pushed his hands away. Her mind spinning, she scuttled to one of the chests lining the wall. She lifted the lid, reached inside, and pulled out fresh clothing.

"I'm sorry." She glanced back at him.

He stood beside the bed, his arms folded and his excitement still evident. "You misunderstood."

"No. I miscalculated."

"What are you doing?"

"What does it look like I'm doing?" she replied from beneath a swirl of periwinkle fabric. "I'm getting dressed."

"Why?"

"'Tis cold in here."

His voice drew nearer. "It seemed warm a moment ago."

Biting her lip, she donned dry stockings and concocted an excuse. "I'll find Tilda and tell her we desire food and a fire." She peeked up at him.

His gaze fell to the boots into which she shoved her feet. "You need only slippers for that."

"She may be in the bailey," she said, fetching a dry veil.

He nodded, but suspicion prowled his features. "My appetite bends in a different direction. But if you're hungry, I wouldn't object to a trencher of food."

Hungry? she thought. Not possible. Her stomach was in knots.

"How about some wine?" she said, securing her headdress. She hurried to the door. "Or a hot bath? Would that please you?"

Grinning like a devil, he glided toward her and put a hand over the door's bolt. "Will you bathe me?"

Heat rushed into her cheeks. "Is that necessary?"

"Very," he said. He ran a finger across her closed lips.

On impulse, she caught his finger between her teeth and gently bit it.

His eyes widened. They seemed darker, more intense. He pulled the finger from between her teeth, then ran it down her chin and throat, stopping at the cleft between her breasts.

"What was that for?" he asked.

"I don't know," she said. 'Twas the truth. She was not herself.

Again, he grinned. Then he unbolted the door and opened it for her. "Don't be long." Her response was a half-hearted smile as she slipped past him into the stairwell. She watched the door close, then stared at the steps which twisted into the darkness below. Just days ago, she'd worried that he'd think her a witch. But perhaps he had a little witchery of his own.

****

Half an hour later, William was still alone in the bedchamber. He had dressed, expecting Tilda's arrival at any moment, but the handmaiden had never come.

Neither had his wife.

He paced the floor, kicking at several unruly, protruding rushes. The speed and consistency with which Emma shrank from his attentions was extraordinary. Calling upon the patience he'd acquired in Hattin's blackest dungeon, he'd accepted her need for a reprieve. He let her leave the chamber, even though the errand was a blatant excuse to get away from him. But the longer he waited, the more her absence smacked of treachery.

He could wait no longer. He threw open the door and descended the stairs, his suspicion increasing with each step. Through narrowed eyes, he searched the great hall and the solar. Only servants occupied the first room; the other was empty.

Intent on scouring all shelters within the curtain wall, he strode to the forebuilding. The patch of sky framed by the stone archway was dingy but dry. The rain had gone into hiding, and that would aid his search.

As he reached the stairs, his jaw tightened. Tilda climbed toward him from the bailey below. Her eyes were so trained to the steps that she didn't notice him until she neared the top. Looking up, she froze.

"Tilda," he said.

"My lord," she managed.

He folded his arms. "Have you seen my wife?"

Tilda assumed the mien of a frightened hare. "Aye," she said.

"Did she speak to you?"

"Briefly."

"And?"

"We thought you were still in the bedchamber."

He tapped his foot. "What did Lady Ravenwood

say?"

"She told me to see to your comfort. I was just on my way to order your bath. Then I'll see to the food and fire."

He nodded. At least Emma had seen the errand through. "Where is she now?"

Tilda's eyes resembled two large chestnuts. "I was to tell you she's busy…that she'll be so for a while."

"Busy?"

"That's what she said."

"Where? Doing what?"

"I don't know."

His tolerance was slipping away. "Don't you?"

She clasped her hands in front of her and shook her head. "No, I swear it."

"When and where did you see her last?"

"A few minutes ago, by the stable."

"Near the gatehouse," he muttered. "But she wouldn't be so foolish as to leave the protection of the keep. Not so soon after the attack."

Tilda cleared her throat. "Begging your pardon, my lord, but her ladyship is capable of anything."

"I'm beginning to see that," he said. Then he stepped past her. "Carry on, Tilda."

The handmaiden's response was lost on a sudden, howling gust of wind. He hustled to the bailey floor and headed toward the gatehouse. Halfway there, a flowing length of periwinkle cloth caught his eye. He stopped and stared.

Flanked on either side by Robert and Guy, Emma approached him. She avoided his eyes. Her cheeks were pink, from either chagrin or the blustery air. He couldn't tell which.

The trio halted in front of him. She met his gaze, and her eyes were bright with defiance. She wasn't sorry at all.

"I've acquired an escort," she said through her teeth.

"So I see," he replied.

Robert's gray eyes mirrored the hue of the sky but held a glint of humor. "Guy and I were in the stable when Lady Ravenwood happened along. We convinced her that a ride through the countryside would be unwise."

"Wiser than traveling on foot," Emma said. "And I would've brought someone with me."

William looked from Robert to Guy. "My thanks to you both."

Robert grinned. "Are you dismissing us?"

William gave him a meaningful look. "My wife and I have matters to discuss…alone."

Robert and Guy exchanged glances. Then they departed without another word.

Emma lifted her chin. "So you found me out."

"I got tired of waiting," William said in a low voice. "What do you mean by slinking off like that?"

"I gave Tilda her orders, just as I said I would."

"It took you long enough."

"She was hard to find."

He gave her a pointed look. "But once you found her, you should've returned to our chamber."

"Where is that law written?" she asked, hands on hips.

"We had an understanding."

"You had one. I needed to breathe."

"I know. That's why I let you go."

Her expression softened, and her arms dropped to her sides. "Oh," she said.

"You needn't fear me, Emma."

"No?"

His gaze locked to hers, he closed the gap between them. "And you mustn't fear yourself. You've a passionate nature, and you cannot run from it."

She raised her eyebrows. "Is that what I'm doing?"

"You know it as well as I."

Her eyes narrowed. "I know only that your conceit is boundless."

"My patience is not. You'd do well to remember that."

"I'll mark it down."

"This too: you could've been hurt if you'd gone riding without a proper escort."

"What would you consider proper? Fifty men?"

"You shouldn't let emotion cloud your judgment."

She cocked her head to the side. "Have you mastered your emotions?"

He straightened his shoulders. "As well as any man."

"That's quite an accomplishment," she said, and her voice dripped sarcasm. "Perhaps your pride is justified."

"If not my pride, then my actions," he said, seizing her hand. "This one, in particular." Pulling her alongside him, he started toward the keep.

"What are you doing?"

"It should be obvious. I'm taking you back to our chamber."

She halted abruptly. "Our chamber?"

He kept a firm grip on her hand. "I honor my

promises. Now you will honor yours."

Her eyes shifted. "Which promise?"

"To bathe me."

She visibly relaxed. "Phew."

"Your enthusiasm is touching."

"I'm sorry, but I don't remember making that promise."

"You have a convenient memory."

"So have you."

He cocked an eyebrow. "Of course, if you'd rather fulfill another promise…"

"No," she said quickly. "A bath is agreeable."

His imagination took flight. He could see her undressing before the fire…could almost feel her straddling him in the warm, soapy water of his bath.

Down, boy, he thought. Then he regarded her. "Would you care to join me?"

She glared at him. "I'll bathe you. Nothing more."

He grinned. *We'll see about that.*

Chapter Thirteen

The bedchamber walls closed in on Emma as she stared at the platter of food. Apples from the orchard, cold duck, cheese, and fresh bread. To wash it down, there was ale. The supper might appeal...if her stomach stopped churning for two seconds together.

She could feel William's gaze on her. Perhaps he was right, and she was running away. She'd never thought of herself as a sexual being. The curse saw to that. So she'd channeled her passion into helping others, unaware that same passion could lead to physical need.

Until William arrived, brandishing raw sensuality which dared her to explore her own.

Frowning, she turned toward the hearth, where eager flames licked firewood and kindling with equal ferocity. In front of the blaze sat a round, wooden tub lined with cloth. Twin brothers—blond, blue-eyed teens who were their mother's pride and joy—filled the tub with hot water, while Tilda placed soap, washrag, and drying cloths on the ground beside it. The handmaiden sent her a sympathetic look over the rim of the tub, then returned to her work.

Too soon, the servants left the chamber, and the door shut behind them with a clunk. William bolted it, then crossed to the tub with long, leisurely steps.

Emma wiped her sweaty palms on her tunic and

cleared her throat. "Aren't you hungry?"

He ran his fingers over the white cloth that lined the tub's edge. "I will be," he answered. "Later."

"Later," she echoed.

He smiled. "Will you undress your husband, or shall I do it myself?"

Her heart fluttered. "You can do it."

He nodded and reached to undo his leather belt. Promptly, she looked away, focusing instead on the window's closed shutters. Her eyes followed the curving design carved into the oak boards.

"Shall I open the window?" she asked.

"'Tis cold out," he replied. "Would you have me ill and in bed again?"

"Not ill," she said, still looking away.

"But in your bed?"

She rolled her eyes. "I see your humor has returned."

"How can you see anything with your back turned?" he countered.

"I'm waiting for you to get into the tub."

"Ah, you dare not look the dragon in the eye."

Despite her nerves, she giggled. "You call it a dragon?"

"When common names fail, one looks to legend."

She snorted. "I suppose it breathes fire."

"It will," he said, his tone suddenly potent, "if you want it to."

An awkward silence followed. She rolled up her sleeves with studied care. Behind her, the swish and rustle of clothing seemed ridiculously loud. At last, she heard the swash of bathwater.

"'Tis safe to turn around," he said.

She turned…and stared.

Framed by the writhing fire and the water lapping at his ribs, he looked at once fiendish and unbearably handsome. She meant to walk forward, but her legs seemed to have lost their mobility.

William grinned. "Does your silence indicate approval or disfavor?"

She blinked and found her voice. "Neither."

"What then?"

"Alarm."

His dark eyes glittered. "Fear not. I promise to behave."

"Behave? I'm afraid to ask your definition of the word."

"'Tis similar to yours, I assure you."

She forced herself to move forward. Her gaze locked onto his and refused to let go, even as she circled the tub.

"Make yourself comfortable," he said.

She made a face and knelt on the pillow beside him. The fire warmed her right side and invaded her cheek.

William leaned back and rested his long arms on the edge of the tub. The bandage on his bicep caught her attention, and she was grateful. It allowed her to assume the familiar role of healer.

"We'll leave this on," she said, ensuring the dressing was tight. "I'll wash around it."

"As you wish."

"By morning, the wound should be ready for cleansing and a new bandage."

His grin deepened. "I'm in your hands."

She pursed her lips, and he raised an eyebrow.

"Wouldn't you like that?" he asked.

She averted her gaze. "Shall I start at the bottom?"

"To which bottom do you refer?"

The fire's heat hounded her, and she began to sweat. "Your feet."

"Oh well. 'Tis a beginning."

She mumbled a string of Saxon oaths and dipped a clean rag into the water. With her other hand, she scooped soft, lavender-scented soap from a jar on the floor. She spread it over the wet cloth, then began to wash his toes.

"You use a different soap," he remarked.

She paused. "I'm surprised you noticed."

"I notice everything."

"Well, I thought you'd rather smell of lavender than of roses."

"Right you are."

She scrubbed the ball of his left foot. "You have big feet."

He chuckled. "True."

She switched to the other foot. "My father had big feet...but a small heart."

"And no sense, if he preferred Gertrude to you."

"Gertrude can be harsh. I doubt she'd bathe you so gently."

"I'd never give her the chance."

Emma slid the washcloth along his left calf. "A wise decision."

He closed his eyes and sighed as she moved to his knee. "My wisest was to have you bathe me."

Her eyes on his face, her brow beaded with sweat, she felt her way to his thigh. His leg tensed, and she faltered.

His eyes shot open. "Why do you stop?"

She licked the salty sweat from her upper lip and stared into his dark eyes. "Your thigh hardened," she said.

He glanced down. "Among other things. Look."

She shook her head. "I can't."

"You can."

"Why must I?"

"Do it, Emma."

She wrenched her gaze from his and lowered it to his full, sensual lips, then to the mat of black hair covering his chest and stomach. At that point, there was no ignoring his proud, engorged manhood.

'Twas larger than she'd expected and almost purple. Even more amazing, it continued to grow.

"Your bath may take longer than anticipated," she said finally.

"Why is that?"

"Every minute there's more of you to clean."

He burst out laughing. "Indeed."

She willed her attention back to his face. "I didn't mean to be funny."

"That's why you were."

She returned his smile. "When you compared yourself to the Long Wood, I thought you were joking."

"When you mentioned horses, I thought you were clever."

"I think 'brave' is the proper word."

"Are you brave enough to face the dragon?" he murmured. He guided her hand up his thigh, but she pulled it away.

Swiftly, she scooted around the tub and knelt behind him. "Your word was better. I'm clever enough to wash a different part of you."

"Which part?"

"Your back, of course. Sit up."

He leaned forward, and her breath caught in her throat. For the first time, she had a clear view of his bare back and the angry scars tangled upon it. Hattin's whip hadn't skimmed William's flesh; it had torn it apart.

Tears stung her eyes. She bent over and kissed one of the scars. Then a second, and a third.

"Emma?" he said.

Blinking back tears, she dropped the rag and placed her hands on his shoulders. "He should burn in Hell."

"Who?"

"The monster that did this to you."

William jerked away from her touch. Slowly, he turned to her. "Of what monster do you speak?"

"Hattin the Horrid."

William's face transformed into a cold, hard mask. "How do you know that name?"

She trembled. "'Twas mentioned once."

"By whom?"

"Your brother."

A muscle worked in his jaw. "How much did he tell you?"

"Enough."

He closed his eyes. "I see."

"He meant well."

"It matters not."

"But it does, William." She swallowed hard. "Maybe if you talked—"

His eyes shot open. "I will not discuss it! Not with you, not with anyone."

"I want to help."

He looked beyond her to the blazing hearth, and his eyes reflected the flames. "Then leave my presence immediately."

She felt rooted to the floor. "What?"

"You heard me." His gaze was riveted on the fireplace, as though the demons that tormented him danced within.

"But—"

"Go!"

Emma jumped to her feet and rushed to the door. Without a backward glance, she left the chamber.

****

William stormed into the solar where Robert stood warming his hands before the fire. In the far corner of the room, Geoffrey and Guy looked up from their game of chess and froze.

"Leave us," William said to the squires.

Robert flinched, then turned to his brother as Geoffrey and Guy scuttled from the room.

"What did you tell her?" William demanded.

"Whom?"

"My wife."

"In Heaven's name, what are you talking about?"

"Heaven has naught to do with it. I'm talking about Hattin."

Robert looked at his leather boots. "Oh."

Heat coursed through William. "Apparently, you've been telling tales."

Robert lifted his gaze in a bold stare. "Only one."

William clenched his fists. "You had no business blurting my history to her."

Robert's expression softened. "Perhaps not, but

147

'twas innocently done."

"There's nothing innocent about betrayal."

"Just listen, William. You were feverish from the arrow's poison and kept babbling Turkish in your sleep. Naturally, she wondered what language you were speaking."

"So you treated her to a bedtime story of treachery and torture."

"She deserved to know. If you'd seen the way she cared for you, you'd agree."

"I'd never agree to sharing my darkest memories."

"You shared them with me."

"Not all of them. I only told you what I could bear to relive."

"Fair enough, but at least you shared something."

"With you, not her."

"How is she any different?"

William crossed his arms. "For one thing, she has a far more appealing shape."

Robert gave him a soulful look. "She's family now."

"She's my wife, and she'll be the mother of my sons. But that is all."

Robert crossed the chamber and dropped onto one of the chairs. "You're as stubborn as she is."

Through narrowed eyes, William studied his brother. "If you were any other man, you'd pay for that comment."

"But I'm not another man, and Lady Ravenwood isn't just another woman. She's got courage, wit, and spirit. Not unlike our mother, in many ways."

William frowned but claimed the chair next to Robert. "But does it follow that she holds the key to my soul?"

Robert shrugged. "In due time, why not?"

"I trod that path long ago. I shall not do so again."

"You speak of Sahar?"

"I do."

"You lost her, aye. But we never learned what really happened."

William glared at him. "I won't discuss it," he hissed through his teeth.

"Too late, Brother. I'm not the only one who knows."

The awful truth dawned. "No," said William. "What possessed you to tell her?"

"You said Sahar's name at least a hundred times while you slept."

"Is nothing of my life sacred to you?"

"Lady Ravenwood was curious."

"Curiosity be damned. You should not have told her."

"What should I have done? Locked her out, as you do?"

"You don't understand."

"But I do, more than you know. We both left a part of ourselves behind in the Holy Land. I lost my faith in God; you lost yours in humanity. Now your wife suffers for it."

William shifted his focus to the blazing hearth. Then he sighed heavily.

He'd hurt Emma by pushing her away. Out of habit, he'd raised the old barriers, the ones so crucial to his sanity and survival in Hattin's dungeon. But he dared not lower them. He couldn't let anyone in. His pain and despair were too bitter, too black. Even for one as strong as Emma.

He looked up from the fire and turned to Robert, who watched him in silence. The next instant, Robert grabbed a pitcher from the table beside him. He poured wine into two cups and handed one to his brother.

"I suppose you stormed out of the bedchamber," Robert said.

William sipped the warm, spiced wine. "Something like that," he muttered.

"Will she let you back in?"

"She can have the chamber to herself. I need space."

"For how long?"

"A few days."

"Where will you sleep?"

"With you."

"Charming, but what of your plans to seduce your wife?"

"They can wait."

"The longer they do, the harder they'll be to achieve."

"I know that."

Robert shrugged and sipped his wine. "Then I guess you know best."

"Always," William replied.

He lifted his gaze to the largest tapestry in the room. Its silken threads depicted lords and ladies dancing around a fire at the edge of a dark wood. William supposed the tapestry paid homage to some sort of pagan ritual. The detail was extraordinary, and the artist who created it had managed to infuse the scene with an unusual sense of movement.

The longer he stared at it, the more the tapestry

came to life. It seemed to whisper and entice. It bade him join in the merriment so vividly portrayed.

But that was foolish, impossible. Magic didn't exist. Even if it did, it could never draw hope from the pit of Hell.

Chapter Fourteen

"Ouch!" Emma glared at the needle that stabbed her and lifted her bleeding thumb to her lips.

Her attempt at embroidery was a miserable failure. All concentration had abandoned her.

Gertrude, however, had not. Unusually quiet, she sat beside Emma on the solar's window seat and stitched her latest masterpiece. Gertrude had a way with needle and thread, much like Emma's grandmother had.

Emma lowered her embroidery hoop to her lap and looked up at the tapestry Meg called "The Forest Dance." 'Twas one of her grandmother's most beautiful creations. As a young girl, Emma had imagined the wall hanging was a whole world of enchantment. For hours, she'd stared at the lively dancers and forest shadows, longing for a spell that could weave her into its magical threads.

Now, as she gazed at the tapestry, the childhood wish returned. Her present reality held no charm. Two days had passed since she argued with William. That meant two sleepless nights during which she'd watched and waited for him to pound on the bedchamber door. He hadn't even knocked.

She glanced out the window at the waning light of day. *I wonder if he'll come knocking tonight,* she thought.

They hadn't spoken or shared the same space since

he ordered her from his bath. She took her meals in the great hall; he dined elsewhere. Even her handmaiden saw more of him, for he'd ordered Tilda to tend his arm until further notice. The arrangement made Emma feel like a leper. She'd stooped to skulking around the castle, spying on him from afar as he bellowed orders to men-at-arms on the battlements and instructed squires practicing combat in the bailey.

'Twas shameful. Ridiculous. And not nearly enough.

At the sound of footsteps, Emma flinched. But 'twas only servants who'd come to light the candles. They went about their work with quick hands and respectful silence. Soon the solar's glow rivaled that of the setting sun, and the servants left the chamber.

The instant they were gone, Gertrude's head snapped up. "You haven't had much luck with your needle." Her green eyes focused on Emma's sore thumb.

"And you haven't had much to say," Emma remarked.

"Oh, I could've said plenty," Gertrude replied. "I didn't think you'd want to hear it."

Emma sighed. "I might as well."

Gertrude planted her needle in her embroidery and set it aside. "There's been talk."

Emma shifted on the hard window seat. "About?"

"Your husband's sleeping arrangements."

Here we go, Emma thought. "Pray continue," she said.

Gertrude folded her arms into a tight bodice. "All of Ravenwood knows you've slept apart the past two nights. The people are worried."

"How does it concern them?"

"They care for you because you care for their ill and broken bodies, though your reasons for doing so are a mystery to me."

Emma frowned. "You sound like my father."

Gertrude sat a little straighter. "He was a good man and a shrewd one."

"So you've said, often."

"He disapproved of your attempts to teach me the healing arts."

"He disapproved of most everything I did."

"Meg wasn't keen on my learning medicine either," Gertrude said, relaxing her arms so her hands fell into her lap "She must've seen how it bored me."

"No doubt."

Gertrude's eyes shone like emeralds. "But I've learned a thing or two about life."

"Such as?"

"The love act is all about pain."

Emma went rigid. "What?"

"I'm not without experience."

"But…when? With whom?"

"It matters not. What does matter is whether or not *you've* gained experience."

Emma's gaze dropped to her needlework. The mangled stitches were just as embarrassing as the memories that surfaced in her mind. She could almost feel William's fingers combing the hair between her legs.

"You're blushing," Gertrude observed.

Emma kept her eyes glued to her muddled embroidery. "What if I am?"

"Has he bedded you?"

"No." Emma glowered at her tender thumb.

Gertrude grunted. "You think your thumb hurts? Just wait until Lord Ravenwood pricks you."

Emma stared at her cousin. "Must you be so crude?"

"I'm only trying to warn you," Gertrude said.

Emma pursed her lips but said nothing. William's caresses were gentle and exciting. But were they worth whatever pain followed?

"Women bear so much discomfort," Gertrude mused. "First, there's the monthly flux, and then our maidenheads are shattered. And how are we rewarded for these trials? The agony of childbirth. Eve must've been wicked indeed for God to invent such torture."

"That fable is man's invention. God wouldn't punish an entire gender because of one mistake."

"You believe that, do you? Well, let me tell you what I believe. The priests accuse Eve of bringing evil into the world because they refuse to take responsibility themselves. If they ever came face to face with her, they'd be frightened out of their skins. They preach against feminine wiles because, deep down, they know any woman with half a brain would run screaming from their advances."

"Don't let Father Cedric hear you say that."

"Let him hear. He could use a shock or two."

"But he's a good man. You know that as well as I."

"My mother was good, too, yet she suffered the same pain we all face. Why?"

"Why indeed?" a male voice rang out from the far side of the room.

Emma's heart fluttered as William entered the solar. His wry grin made her wonder just how much of the conversation he'd heard.

Gertrude lifted her chin. "How long have you been standing there?"

"Long enough," he replied. "You've raised an interesting question about what women experience."

Gertrude tossed her long, chestnut braid over her shoulder. "I suppose you have an answer."

"I have a guess," said William. "Perhaps the pain balances out the tremendous pleasure women feel during lovemaking."

"'Tis no more than a man's pleasure," Gertrude retorted.

William's smile grew. "In intensity, maybe not. But there's something to be said for repetition."

Gertrude made a face. "You are misinformed."

His smile vanished. "I don't know who's been schooling you, Gertrude, but he's obviously a poor lover."

Gertrude snatched up her embroidery and stood. "I'm leaving."

"A pity," said William.

In a huff, Gertrude marched out of the solar. William grinned unrepentantly.

"I believe you've made a friend," Emma said dryly.

"I only hope I haven't lost one."

"Meaning?"

He crossed his arms. "I was rude to you the other night."

"Aye. You were."

"I was angry with my brother."

"And with me, it seemed."

"'Twas more growl than grievance."

An awkward hush fell between them. William shifted his weight from one foot to the other.

"And?" said Emma.

He unfolded his arms. "And what?"

She cocked her head to the side. "Forgive me, but I thought you were apologizing."

"Oh," he said. Then he clasped his hands behind his back. "I'm sorry."

She hesitated, then gave him a nod of acceptance. "Better late than never, I suppose."

"There have been demands on my time."

"And you needed space, just as I did the other day."

He regarded her in silence. "Perhaps I did," he said at last.

"Will you need space tonight?"

His face brightened. "No. We'll sup together."

"In the hall?"

"In our bedchamber."

Her stomach quivered. "Oh," she said.

He stepped closer. "Afterward, I'll return a favor that's long overdue."

"What favor is that?"

"The excellent bath you gave me."

She blinked. "You're going to bathe me?"

"I am. 'Twill be painless, I assure you."

She raised her eyebrows and gave him a dubious look.

"You doubt me?" he asked.

She shook her head. "Not exactly. I just feel a bit..."

"Anxious?"

"Like a lamb to the slaughter."

He chuckled. "How would you feel if you did doubt me?"

She crinkled her nose. "Well…"

"Don't answer that. Just come with me."

****

In the warmth and privacy of their bedchamber, William observed his wife. She wore red, and the color suited her. However hard she tried to curb her passion, 'twas there, waiting to be unleashed. As she stared down at her half-eaten supper, the fire's glow enhanced her delicate features, yet softened the thin creases on her forehead. Somehow, he had to help her relax.

"Not hungry?" he said.

Startled, Emma looked up. "No," she murmured.

He gazed into her wide, violet eyes and renewed his determination to woo her. 'Twould take every ounce of his patience and skill, but he had to succeed. And he would.

She glanced at his empty trencher. "Your appetite thrives, I see."

"Aye." He pushed his chair back from the table. "I need sustenance to perform my duties."

"You mean my bath?"

"That is no duty. 'Tis a pleasure."

"One you could easily forego."

"I think not."

"I was afraid you'd say that."

He grinned. "Shall I call the servants?"

"Let me," she said, standing. Her lips performed a nervous twitch which might've been meant as a smile. "I must excuse myself for a moment anyway."

He stood and skirted the edge of the table so there was no barrier between them. "Why?"

"I must visit the garderobe."

"Are you unwell?"

"Oh, no. Just heeding the call of nature."

He studied her face and wondered if she'd run away again. But he had to let her go. Trust was essential to any working relationship.

He nodded. "Very well."

She skittered past him and disappeared down the stairs. Not five minutes later, four servants filed into the chamber. They cleared away food, prepared the bath, and kept their eyes on their work all the while. William's eyes watched the doorway. He saw only shadows, phantoms created by the flickering torches that lined the stairwell.

When all of the servants had gone and his patience had begun to waver, he heard at last the light pat of slippered feet climbing the stairs. Then he sighed with satisfaction as Emma appeared in the doorway.

"I was beginning to feel your absence," he said.

She seemed rooted to the threshold. "I lost track of time," she said. "Again."

He laughed. "'Tis a sad state when you prefer the garderobe to my company."

"I wouldn't say that."

"Well, before you say anything else, come in and shut the door. Your bathwater won't stay warm forever."

She nodded and slid the thick, oak bolt in place. Then she turned and regarded him through narrowed eyes.

"Well?" he said.

"I have a request to make," she said.

He smiled. "Perhaps you'd like to be washed

gently or rubbed in a particular place."

Her blush rivaled her red dress. "You're not making this easy."

"No, but I'm having fun."

"Obviously."

"I'm listening, though. Pray continue."

She cleared her throat. "I'm ready to undress and let you bathe me, but you should remember our discussion."

"Which one?"

"The one about the curse. You must promise to behave."

He grinned. Her tenacity was second to none. "I promise."

"Good. You are a man of your word."

"And you are still woefully clad."

She gave him a look drenched with meaning, then settled onto a stool. Carefully, she removed her headdress and unbraided her lustrous hair. It flowed down her back and swayed at her hips with the dark, velvet promise of midnight. Casting a glance at the tub, she pulled off her slippers and stockings…and gave him a tantalizing glimpse of her calves.

She continued to avoid his gaze as she stood again. She doffed her overtunic, then wriggled out of her inner tunic. All that remained was her thin, linen smock.

She hesitated and met his gaze. "Do you have to drool?"

He raised a hand to his mouth. "I feel no moisture."

"You know what I mean."

"I do, but don't blame me. If you weren't so lovely, I wouldn't be obliged to look."

She smiled. Then her hands found her hips. "I think

you delight in catching me off-guard."

"I'd be more delighted if you were nude. Come now, remove your chemise. Your bathwater grows cold."

She took a deep breath and gathered the sides of her smock. Slowly, she pulled the garment over her head.

His breath caught in his throat. She was perfect. Her legs were long and shapely. At their apex, black curls shone like silken midnight against her creamy white skin. Her full hips tapered to a small waist; her rounded breasts to taut, pink nipples.

His manhood hardened. He was speechless.

"William?" she said.

He ripped his gaze from her breasts and sought her amethyst eyes. "Aye," he rasped.

"Remember your promise."

He willed his blood to cool. Then he nodded.

She threw her hair over her breasts in an apparent effort to hide her nakedness. But as she hurried to the cloth-lined tub and stepped inside it, her bare back gave William an exquisite view of her curvaceous bottom. He licked his lips and sauntered toward the tub.

Immersed in bathwater, Emma hugged her knees to her chest and gave him a shy smile. "'Tis still warm," she said.

"Is it?" He imagined her flesh would feel even warmer locked around his manhood, but he banished the thought as soon as it came. Control was crucial.

"Aye, thankfully," she said.

The roaring fire beyond the tub was too hot for William, so he started to remove his clothes. With each garment that fell to the floor, Emma's eyes grew larger.

When only his breeches remained, he knelt beside the tub. "Better," he said.

"How so?" she croaked.

He grabbed the jar of soap and breathed in the scent of rose petals. "I was too warm."

"Oh," she said, still clutching her knees.

He gave her the gentlest smile he could muster. "Your knees make a poor shield, Emma. Your bath will be easier and quicker if you relax."

Nodding, she released her knees and slid her legs under the water.

He fought the urge to caress her heaving breasts. The left one was slightly larger than the right, its pink tip even riper for his touch.

He cleared his throat. "Shall we start with your hair?"

Again, she nodded. She seemed to have lost the power of speech, but not her inherent grace. Gliding forward in the tub, she arched her back and submerged her hair in the water. The movement was beautiful, natural, and incredibly sensual. Her hard nipples pointed skyward, and he clenched his free hand into a fist to keep from reaching out to them.

She lifted her head with the same slow, catlike elegance. Suppressing a savage curse, he plunged his fingers into the soft soap. He ignored his arousal and focused instead on lathering her wet hair.

As his fingers massaged her scalp, she closed her eyes. "Mmm," she hummed.

The sound was like music. "You see?" he said. "There's naught to fear."

Rhythmically and thoroughly, he washed her hair. Then he grabbed a ewer from the floor and poured. She sighed as the warm water cascaded over her hair and down her back.

He grinned. "You're easy to please."

Her eyes opened. "Am I?"

"You take pleasure in the simplest things."

"I suppose I do. Textures, scents, sensations. The way a fruit feels in my mouth is just as important as how it tastes."

"I understand, but you'd be amazed how many don't."

She frowned. "It seems wasteful to shun our senses. They should be savored."

Exactly, he thought. She was a child of nature, a champion of sensation. And she'd just voiced his thoughts with uncanny precision.

Her cheeks flooded with color. "I didn't mean...that is to say..."

"I know," he said. "Let's continue with your bath."

He doused a clean rag, lifted her hair, and scrubbed her back. Then he smeared soap on the rag and washed her feet.

"Such tiny toes," he commented.

"Tinier than yours, at any rate."

"By a mile." He slid the washrag from her left ankle to her calf. The flesh was soft and supple, a foretaste of pleasures to come.

He swallowed hard and moved to her knee. His attentions there were brief, for he couldn't resist pushing the washcloth higher. Almost before he realized it, the cloth waded to the bottom of the tub, and his bare hand massaged her thigh.

She seized the washrag. "I'd better do the next bit."

His hand inched higher. "To which bit do you

refer?"

She clapped her hand over his. "You know very well."

His eyes bored into hers. "But this is your bath. You should relax and let me do the work."

"I'd rather do it myself."

He nodded and removed his hand from her thigh with exaggerated care. But he couldn't remove his gaze from her hand as she slid the washcloth between her legs.

She ignored his stare while she washed herself but looked up when she finished. She handed him the rag. "You're drooling again," she muttered.

He took the washrag and kissed it. "I've a right to," he murmured against the cloth.

She blushed. "You may continue."

His heart leapt. "With my kiss?"

"With my bath."

Battling his excitement, William added more soap to the rag and began to wash Emma's stomach. He dipped the cloth into her navel, and she giggled.

"So you're ticklish there," he said with a grin.

"Mayhap," she replied.

He wiggled his index finger in the tiny hole, and she laughed out loud. 'Twas a beautiful sound.

"Tell the truth," he said, tickling her still.

"Aye," she admitted. "Now please stop!"

He relented and slid the washcloth up her belly to the valley between her breasts. Casually, he slipped the cloth beneath her left breast, then circled to the top. She gasped as it moved across the nipple.

"Perhaps I should wash this part as well," she said.

"No," he insisted. "This part is mine."

Through the thin cloth, he felt her pap harden. He moved the rag in a circular motion, lingering on the nipple as long as he dared.

With effort, he tore his gaze from the flushed peak to observe Emma's expression. She bit her lip, resisting her passion, even as he inflamed it.

Go ahead, he thought, *fight me. But before this night is through, you will know your true nature.*

He shifted the washcloth to the other breast. Emma clamped her mouth shut and stared straight ahead. Her hands gripped the edge of the tub.

After prying her fingers loose, he washed her left arm and then her right. His final stop was her long neck. Then he threw the rag into the soapy water.

She regarded him. "Finished?"

He smiled. "I could scrub your bottom."

"You've done quite enough. Now, if you'll hand me a drying cloth, I'll get out."

"My lady," he said with a bow. He unfolded a large cloth, then stood and held it outstretched.

She rose quickly amid a swash of water. Then she wrapped the cloth around her, covering everything from the top of her breasts to the middle of her thighs.

Lamenting the size of the drying cloth, he took her hand and helped her from the tub. "Shall I comb your hair?" he offered.

She sat before the hearth. "Thank you, but I can do it."

He crossed the chamber and leaned against the bed. Entranced, he watched Emma work the tangles from her hair. The fire in the hearth seemed an inferno which might devour her at any moment.

No, he thought with a grin. *That's my job.*

165

"Emma," he said.

She pushed her straight, combed hair away from her face and looked at him. "Aye?"

"Come to me."

"Why?"

He rubbed his hands together. "I have a craving for sweetmeat."

Chapter Fifteen

Emma tried and failed to keep her gaze from William's bare chest. Between his hungry eyes and the fur coverlets, he looked like a primitive hunter. Why that appealed, she couldn't fathom.

"You want a sweetmeat?" she asked.

His teeth gleamed. "I need one."

"I'm surprised you've a stomach for it after the supper you consumed."

"My appetite is insatiable at times."

Her nipples still tingled from his exploits with the washrag. Hugging the drying cloth, she stood. "Perhaps I should dress and call one of the servants."

"There's no need."

"But I see no sweetmeats about. Did you hide them somewhere?"

"Actually, you did."

She frowned. "I don't understand."

His eyes were as black as the moonless night outside. "The sweetmeat I want is hidden beneath that cloth."

Suspicion dawned. "You mean my body?"

"Part of it."

"Which part?"

"You'll see."

"I don't wish to."

He stood to his full height and folded his arms.

"Emma."

Clutching her comb, she stepped backward. The fire's heat reached out for her. The flames hissed and whispered at her back, snapping kindling with unmitigated ease. The hearth was alive...and ardent.

"I know your fears, and I'll respect them," William said. "I told you before, there are other things we can do. You must trust me."

But can I trust myself? she wondered.

"I want to," she said aloud.

He unfolded his arms. "Then come to me."

She took a deep breath, then exhaled slowly. *Enough of this dithering by the fire,* she scolded herself. *Are you a woman or a child? Go.*

She set the comb on the stool, then pushed back her shoulders. With head held high, she crossed the chamber and halted in front of him. He towered over her. Dark, powerful, and handsome as the night was long.

He gazed into her eyes. Into her soul.

"If at any moment my touch displeases you, you must tell me," he said.

"So be it," she replied. In one quick movement, she removed the drying cloth and dropped it on the floor.

His eyes flared. Swiftly, he lifted her in his arms and laid her on the bed. One moment, he stood looking down at her, burning her naked flesh with his stare. The next, he lay beside her.

He leaned over her. "Emma," he breathed.

The furs beneath her body were soft, but his kiss was softer. His tongue teased her lips, daring them to open. They parted eagerly, and she invited his tongue with her own.

He groaned and kissed her with such ardor her head spun. She breathed in his intoxicating scent and slipped her arms around him. Her heart swelled as she ran her hands over the maze of scar tissue on his back. She pulled him closer and intensified the kiss.

He drank from her lips as though dying of thirst and blazed a trail of kisses from her cheek to her earlobe. Then he darted his tongue into her ear, and she shivered.

His deep voice vibrated in her ear. "Does it please you?"

She swallowed hard. "Aye."

"Then I'll continue."

He probed her ear again, and his tongue sent chills along every inch of her flesh. His lips explored her neck, then the hollow of her throat. They brushed her left nipple and closed over the hard pap. He drew on it gently at first, then harder until she trembled. Unconsciously, she raised a hand to her right breast.

William looked up. "Well," he murmured, pushing her hand aside. "We mustn't deprive the other."

He grazed her right nipple with his teeth, then sucked it until she moaned with pleasure. In response, he ran his tongue down her torso and dipped it into her navel.

"Oh!" she cried.

"You like that?"

"It tickles."

"That's the idea."

He tongued the navel again and continued until she giggled uncontrollably.

"My job here is done," he said. "Now for my sweetmeat."

She froze. "Is that what you meant?"

"Aye, and my hunger has only grown."

Heat suffused her cheeks. "'Tis unthinkable."

He kissed her belly halfway between the navel and the dark triangle below it. "Oh, I thought about it during your entire bath," he murmured against her skin.

Her stomach fluttered. "You cannot."

"Watch me."

"But—"

"Emma," he interrupted. "I told you, I'll stop if my touch displeases you."

Her mouth was dry. She licked her lips. "It does. I know already."

He shook his head. "Sorry. You can only protest after I've tried it."

"That doesn't seem fair."

"The injustice of the world is a subject for scholars. It has no place here."

"What about chivalry?"

He grinned. "Believe me, this is a noble quest."

"But you'll stop if I ask you to?" she said, placing a hand on his bicep.

He kissed the hand, then gave her a look that was at once confident and wicked. "I will, but you won't ask."

She considered her options. There were none. "Very well," she said in a shaky voice.

He licked his lips. "Spread your legs."

"William—"

His gaze held hers. "You've enjoyed my other caresses, haven't you?"

"I have."

"Did I hurt you in any way?"

She shook her head. "No."

"Then trust me again."

She shut her eyes against her embarrassment and spread her legs a few inches. He chuckled, and she opened her eyes.

"Wider," he instructed.

"How much?"

"Pretend you're riding a horse."

"I ride sidesaddle."

He planted a kiss on her hip. "You are stubborn. Allow me."

She bit her lip as he opened her legs and positioned himself between them. She felt horribly exposed.

"Relax," he said.

Her response was a nervous laugh.

"I'm serious," he declared.

"I'm sure you are," she said. Then she sighed. "I'll try."

He bent down. "That's all I ask."

Leisurely, he kissed the insides of both her thighs. Then he blew on the black curls between them. She wriggled under the cool sensation.

"Your scent is paradise," he murmured.

She gasped and started to close her legs, but his hands prevented her.

"Don't," he said, nuzzling closer. "You're perfect."

She doubted she was any such thing, but the thought that he believed it warmed her. She smiled. Then, as his fingers parted the hair that was her last shield against him, she tensed.

"Ah," he crooned. "You're already wet."

"Is that bad?"

"Just the opposite."

Her legs twitched as his tongue traced her nether lips. Hot and moist, the caress sent a trickle of pleasure from the tender flesh to the pit of her stomach. Never had she imagined such an intimate kiss.

"I was right," he rasped. "You taste of honey."

"I—"

"Salty and sweet."

"William, are you sure this is wise?"

He looked up. "Does it give you pleasure?"

Her cheeks burned. "Aye."

"Then 'tis wise enough."

He lowered again to her silken folds. His exploration was slow and thorough. She closed her eyes and surrendered to it.

Gently, his tongue pushed against the tiny bud of her desire. Her eyes flew open.

"Blessed Virgin," she whispered.

"Indeed you are," he teased.

Softly, skillfully, he flicked his tongue back and forth over the nubbin. The motion was slow at first, but grew steadily faster. She closed her eyes and writhed beneath him. The exquisite, tingling sensation that began as a trickle had become a storm.

William groaned and became more insistent. He lowered his mouth to her nether lips and thrust his tongue inside.

She whimpered. In desperation, she lifted her hips and clutched the furs that cushioned her.

He returned his tongue to the bud of her passion, increasing the pressure and speed of his caress. Her breath quickened. She tossed her head on the pillow as her whole being focused on the sweet assault.

A sudden jolt of intense pleasure coursed through

her. She arched her body and cried out. "William!"

****

Basking in Emma's exotic scent, William smiled. She'd called his name. He felt a deep satisfaction which made him want to please her even more.

The things I could teach her, he thought. *The pleasure we might share.*

He wanted to bury himself inside her and make her shout his name again. But that must wait. She needed time to become accustomed to his touch, and his appetite.

Through a haze of desire, he kissed her hot mound once more, then shifted to lie beside her. He propped his head in his hand and savored the sight of her flushed, voluptuous body. It glistened with sweat and beckoned him like magic. Unable to help himself, he slid his hand over the smooth, flawless skin of her belly.

Emma stretched her limbs luxuriously and sighed. Then she turned to him. "Thank you."

He grinned. "'Twas my pleasure, as well."

"Truly?"

"Aye."

Her violet eyes sparkled. "I never imagined such a feeling."

He moved his hand to the soft curve of her hip. "It must be experienced firsthand."

She nodded. "Now I understand why lovemaking dominates men's thoughts."

"Women's, too."

"I suppose I shall dwell on it after tonight."

He chuckled. She was deliciously frank. "There are worse fates," he commented.

Her gaze fell to his braies, and she stared. "Is that one of them?" she asked, pointing.

He was all too aware of his erection. It seemed mammoth. "You might say that." He removed his hand from her hip to loosen the string of his breeches.

All at once, she rolled toward him and reached for his little finger. With a slow, feather-light touch, she slid her fingertips along its unnaturally twisted length.

Dark memories fought with the pleasure of the caress. "Why are you doing that?" he questioned.

"To take away some of the hurt you've felt," she said softly.

"But why would you wish to?"

"You are my husband. Your pain is mine."

Her answer melted his resistance. He watched her thumb and forefinger move up and down the crooked finger. Little by little, desire overshadowed memory.

"Emma," he said.

Her eyes claimed his. "Aye?"

"There is one way you could ease my torment."

"What is it?"

"Do you remember the tension that built in your body as I kissed it?"

Her cheeks colored. "I do."

"The rush of pleasure you felt was the release of that tension. My body feels the same pressure, but it hasn't been released."

Her hand hesitated. "What must I do?"

"You could stroke my manhood as you do my finger."

The blush spread to her forehead. "And you would feel the pleasure I did?"

He could still taste her on his lips. "I would," he

said.

"Then I shall try."

Every nerve in his body stood at attention. Quickly, he untied his breeches and removed them. Then he stretched out on his back.

She gaped at the sight of his member. "You're enormous!"

"Thank you, my dear."

"The pressure inside you must be great."

"To say the least."

She cleared her throat. "Tell me what to do," she said.

"Grab hold of it."

"Like this?"

He gritted his teeth as her cool fingers closed around him. "Aye."

She squeezed him gently. "How hot you are!"

"You've no idea."

"I moved up and down your finger. Should I do that here?"

"Please."

She loosened her grip and stroked his shaft from base to tip. He tensed and sucked in his breath.

She stilled. "Did I hurt you?"

"God no."

"Oh. Good."

She released the shaft and circled its tip with her finger. He moaned and squeezed his eyes shut.

"How smooth," she purred, repeating the motion. "'Tis fascinating."

"Emma," he said tightly.

"What?"

"Stroke me."

She nodded and caressed him in earnest. Her hand was like silk. Her scent, divine.

He thought he would die of pleasure. He'd held back for so long, and she was his angel of mercy.

"Harder," he said. "Faster."

She stroked his throbbing member with single-minded focus. His heart pounded in his chest. He rode a tempest of sensation that was about to come crashing down.

He bucked his hips on a burst of pleasure so extreme it blinded him for a moment. Hot juices spurted from his body as he growled his release.

"Oh!" she cried, still stroking him.

He shuddered and covered her hand with his. "Enough," he said.

She pulled her hand away. "So that's your seed," she said. "There's a lot of it. Shall I fetch a washcloth."

"Aye."

He closed his eyes and listened to the soft crunch of rushes under her feet. Never had he felt so content, so complete. He sighed, then gave in to a great yawn.

"Tired?" She returned with the cloth.

"Very." He wiped away the evidence of their lovemaking.

She stood beside the bed, hugging her torso. "I'm cold."

He pulled back the fur coverlets and the smooth, linen sheet and nestled under them. "I'll warm you," he said. "Hop in."

Beneath the covers, he gathered her in his arms. She pressed her nose against his collarbone; it felt like ice.

"You are cold," he said.

"I'm sorry," she said, lifting her head. "I'll warm up soon."

He kissed the tip of her nose. "No matter."

She laid her head on his chest, and he pulled her closer. He relished the feel of her softness against him. Their bodies fit together perfectly.

"William?" she said.

"Mmm?"

A long pause followed. "Nothing," she said at last.

He ran his fingers through her satiny, raven hair. "Are you certain?"

She rubbed her cheek against his chest. "Aye," she said. "Certain."

"Good night, then."

"Good night."

Sleep well, Raven, he thought. He closed his eyes and within minutes, he was asleep.

He dreamt that night of the tapestry in the solar. His dream-self gazed up at it when suddenly, a musical sigh lilted toward him from behind. He turned to see Emma floating wraithlike through the doorway. Her body was luminous, transparent. She drifted toward him and took his hand. Her touch seemed more spirit than flesh.

In a flash, he was weightless, rising above the floor.

"Come." Her voice was strange, resonant, like the strain of a harp intoning several notes at once.

Together, they floated toward the tapestry and entered its world. The forest was black. The fire roared. Laughing and singing, the revelers danced around the flames.

"Come," Emma said in the same powerful, ethereal

voice.

"No," he said. "I shan't."

She stretched her arms wide, as though summoning the forces of heaven and hell. "You shall!" she boomed.

He tried to push her away, but his hands went right through her. He recoiled and turned to the forest. Its dark, forbidden depths beckoned him. There he'd be safe. There he could remain just as he was.

Comfortable. Certain. Cold.

Carried on the whistling wind, he floated toward the forest.

Chapter Sixteen

"You're unusually quiet this morning," Meg said. She looked up from the neat piles of herbs which covered the table in Emma's workshop.

Emma lifted a posy of heather to her nose and breathed in its sweet fragrance. "I know."

"Do you want to take a break?" Meg asked.

Emma gazed at the purple flowers in her hand. "No."

"Do you want me to find Tilda so she can help us?"

"No."

"Well, what do you want?"

Emma placed the heather on the worktable and turned to Meg. "That's the trouble," she said. "I don't know."

Meg tilted her head, and her violet eyes narrowed. "Maybe you do, and you just won't admit it."

"To admit our desires is to give them power over us."

"Clever words, Emma, but do you truly believe them?"

"I believe that wanting too much from life leads to pain and disappointment."

"Not so. Desire is a good thing. It leads to action, and action designs destiny."

A familiar shadow crept into Emma's mind. "What if my destiny is to die?"

Meg raised her hand to Emma's cheek. "Everyone dies, child."

"I know, but I'd like to live as long as possible."

"Well, brooding in silence has never strengthened anyone's health. Tell me what's wrong."

Emma's stomach quivered. "I feel strange inside, like something is missing."

"Go on," said Meg.

Emma glanced at her gold wedding band and ran a finger over its smooth surface. "I never sought marriage," she said. "When I learned of King Henry's edict, I prayed my husband would be a kind, strong man bent on peace. I hoped he would respect my wish to remain chaste."

"Then Lord Ravenwood arrived." Meg leaned against the table.

"Exactly."

"And things changed."

Emma reached for the mortar on the table, but at the last second, she withdrew her hand. With resolve, she turned to Meg. "*I've* changed."

"How so?"

"I'm beginning to care for him, and I find myself wanting..."

"Love?"

Emma nodded. "But not just the physical kind. It must be emotional and spiritual, as well."

Meg regarded her for a long moment. Her shrewd eyes missed nothing. "Are you sure this desire is new?"

"If not, where has it been hiding?" Emma asked, frowning.

"In your heart, perhaps. Your dreams. Buried so deep you hardly recognize it now."

Emma shifted her weight from one foot to the other. "You could be right."

Meg straightened, and her eyes twinkled. "I know I am."

"What makes you so certain?"

"Experience."

"Have you known love?" Emma asked. The idea was surprising, and intriguing.

"I have," Meg answered. "One day I'll tell you about it."

"Why not today?"

"Your relationship is more pressing."

With a rueful grin, Emma nodded. "You have a point."

Meg looked thoughtful. "'Tis odd, though. In a way, the curse mirrors the wish you've concealed all these years. True love, or none at all."

"I suppose I *am* given to extremes," Emma said.

Meg raised an eyebrow. "That's putting it mildly."

"Couldn't there be a compromise? Could the love that breaks the curse be one-sided?"

"On your side, you mean?"

"Aye."

Meg shook her head. "The legend is clear. It must be a shared love, deep and true."

Emma's heart sank. "Then there's little hope."

"You said you're beginning to care for Lord Ravenwood. That's a start."

"But how can I make him care for me?"

"Love cannot be forced. It must come of its own."

"If it came to Lord Ravenwood, he'd probably scare it away. He's a hard man, Meg. He's had to be."

"I'm sure, but don't lose heart. Your desire for love

was hidden deep, yet it existed. Perhaps, even now, there's a part of your husband that's reaching out to you."

Abruptly, Emma recalled William's stiff, proud manhood in her hand. Heat rushed into her cheeks.

"Not that part," Meg said with a sly grin. "Something less tangible."

Emma's eyes widened. "You read my thoughts with frightening ease."

"I sense your frustration, too."

"I wonder if my husband does."

"You're probably as much a mystery to him as he is to you."

"Well, I hate hovering in limbo, having to guess the workings of his heart. Is there nothing I can do to sway his affections?"

"In the end, he must love you for yourself."

Emma's gaze dropped to her boots. "Not even my father could do that."

"The people love you."

Emma regarded Meg. "Not for myself."

Meg put her hands on her hips. "For what then?"

"My skills as a healer."

"You're wrong, Emma."

"I think not." She turned toward the table.

Meg patted Emma's arm. "Well, I love you."

With a sad smile, Emma turned back to her. "Aye, but you're different."

Meg folded her arms. "Really? Lord Ravenwood's heart may turn out to be no different from mine."

Emma grunted. "Now you speak of miracles."

"Not necessarily. Time can soften a man's memories and teach him to love."

"How many moons must I wait for this grand transformation?"

"As many as it takes."

Emma sighed. "You're right. And in the meantime, I protect my virginity. 'Tis the only way."

Meg glanced at the herbs on the worktable. "There may be another," she said slowly. "I've taught you all I know about healing, but there's preventive medicine, as well."

Emma perked up. "Do you know a way to prevent conception?"

"There's a little-known drink that contains dittany and rue. It might work. But it must be taken several hours before coupling, and the measurements must be exact."

"I'm sure. Too much rue is poisonous."

"I know the proper amount, but even so, the medicine could fail."

Emma bit her lip and considered the risks involved. They were too great. "I dare not rely on it," she said. "I must keep Lord Ravenwood's passion at bay."

Gertrude appeared in the doorway. "That won't be easy."

"I don't suppose it will," Emma replied. "Why are you here?"

Gertrude rolled her eyes. "Your husband has sent me on an errand. Apparently, he suffers under the delusion that I'm his servant."

"Hate sours your complexion, Gertrude," Meg said coolly. "There's no room for delusion in a man of Lord Ravenwood's mold."

Gertrude made a face. "I see he has an advocate."

"He has two," Emma said. "Now, what is your

errand?"

Gertrude turned to Meg. "Lord Ravenwood wishes to speak with you."

"Me?" said Meg. "Why?"

Gertrude shrugged. "I'm not a soothsayer. He awaits you in the solar."

Meg laid her hand on Emma's shoulder. "Can you finish without me?"

"Of course," said Emma. "Go."

Meg's smile was warm and reassuring. "Keep faith, Emma."

"I'll try," Emma replied.

Meg brushed past Gertrude and marched into the sunlight.

Emma frowned. Why had William summoned Meg? What could they possibly have to talk about?

Me, she thought.

Gertrude stepped into the workshop. "Meg is showing her age."

"You must be joking," Emma said. "We'd be lucky to boast of half her energy."

Gertrude approached the table. "You're probably right. I just said it because I'm in a foul temper."

"Why?"

"I overheard your conversation."

"I see."

"No, you don't. I know I'm disagreeable at times, but I do care about you."

"I know."

Gertrude lowered her gaze. "And I worry for you."

"You needn't. I worry enough for us both."

Gertrude looked up again. Her green eyes brimmed with emotion. "But are you thinking clearly?"

Emma turned to the table and stared at the small, fragrant heaps atop it. "At the moment, I've no wish to think about anything but my work."

Gertrude stepped closer. "What are you doing, anyway?"

"Replenishing my stock."

"Since Meg's gone to face your husband, I can help you."

Emma turned to her. "I could use the help, but are you sure you want to?"

"Why wouldn't I?"

"You've never shown an interest in the healing arts."

"That may be true, but you need help. And you'd be astonished how much I remember. Any herbs I don't recognize, you can tell me."

"Very well." Emma grabbed a jar from one of the shelves. "Let's begin."

Gertrude cleared her throat. "Before we do, I've one last piece of advice."

Emma placed the jar on the worktable and sighed. "Is it brief?"

"Aye."

"Then go ahead."

Gertrude glanced toward the door as though wary of being overheard. "Take care, Cousin. Lord Ravenwood has already seized your land. Now he could steal your heart. After that, there's only one thing left to take."

"What is that?" Emma asked, but she already knew the answer.

Gertrude leaned forward. "Your life."

****

"You sent for me?"

The clear, resonant voice startled William. He pulled his gaze from the vibrant tapestry and turned to see Meg standing beside the empty fireplace. Her gray clothing reminded him of a stealthy mist. The old woman certainly moved like one. How she'd entered the solar undetected was a mystery.

"I did," he said, folding his arms.

Meg glanced at the tapestry behind him. "I see you've noticed 'The Forest Dance.'"

"How could I not?"

She nodded. "It holds a peculiar fascination for many."

"Who made it?"

"Emma's grandmother. She was a gifted weaver."

"Evidently."

A fay twinkle brightened her eyes. "What's less evident is the tapestry's true nature."

"Which is?"

"Magic."

He snorted. "'Tis but color and thread. Nothing more."

Meg was solemn and preternaturally still. "No," she said. "When you look into the tapestry, it looks into you."

He stared at her for a long moment. "Ridiculous," he said at last.

She cocked her head to the side as Emma so often did. "Have you seen the tapestry of the boar's hunt in the storeroom below?"

He thought back to his first day at Ravenwood, when John, the steward, led him down the hidden stairs. "I have," he said. "Emma's grandmother made it too?"

"She did. At one time, it hung in the hall, but Emma's father had it moved."

"For what reason?"

"It gave him nightmares."

Images from his dream the night before flashed through his mind. "Oh?"

"As the tapestries are woven, so too they weave."

He frowned. "Explain."

"They enhance a person's inner world. Hopes and fears, choices one must make."

He shifted his weight from one foot to the other and looked to the hearth. 'Twas dormant, cold. A sense of foreboding crept into his awareness, but he rebuffed it.

He returned his attention to Meg. "You'll understand if I remain skeptical," he said.

"Of course," she said calmly, "but the truth remains. The daughters of Ravenwood are blessed with extraordinary gifts."

"Emma mentioned her visions, and you've explained her grandmother's talent. What is yours?"

"Do you really want to know?"

"Would I have asked otherwise?"

She regarded him in silence for several seconds. Then she lifted her chin. "Dreams," she said.

He clasped his hands behind his back. "Prophetic ones?"

"At times, but prophecy is not always what it seems. My dreams have shown me that the past, present, and future are one."

"You speak in riddles."

"I speak from experience."

"Would you care to elaborate?"

"Not today, but I would ask you a question."

"This should be interesting," he muttered.

She took a step closer. "Have you ever had a dream that was so real you weren't sure it *was* a dream?"

"When I awoke, you mean?"

"Whether we wake or merely shift between realities is an old puzzle, but for our purposes, aye. When you awoke."

His eyes narrowed. "Once, maybe twice. Why?"

"My dreams are always real, in one way or another. 'Tis like entering a parallel world that shimmers with secret information."

"Such as?"

"What I dreamt last night. Perhaps you can help me translate it."

"How could I help?"

"I dreamt of you."

His fingers twitched behind his back. "What saw you?"

"You fought a serpent with your sword. The creature was large and powerful, but the most striking thing was its color."

"So what color was this serpent?"

"Blue."

A dark memory slithered through his mind, but he said nothing.

"Why was it blue?" she asked. "Do you know?"

His hands tightened their grip. "I may."

"Pray tell."

"No. I'll not discuss it."

Meg studied his face and posture. "Then perhaps you'll discuss your reason for summoning me."

He relaxed his hands and dropped them to his

sides. "I have questions about the curse. I know Lady Ravenwood believes in it, but I want a second opinion. And I want the truth."

"You've already heard the truth from Emma. The curse is real."

"I took you for a practical person."

"I am practical, but I also leave room for magic. A fruitful life balances both."

"The only fruit that interests me is what would grow in Lady Ravenwood's womb."

"Strong words for a man who threw himself in front of a poisoned arrow."

"I didn't know 'twas poisoned."

"But you knew 'twould hurt Emma. Which reminds me, have you learned anything more about the attack?"

He shook his head. "My men found nothing within a day's ride of Ravenwood, but they're keeping watch. Why do you ask?"

She shivered. "'Tis only a feeling I have."

"You sense danger."

"Aye, and so do you."

A silent understanding bridged the space between them. Their bond was a mutual desire to protect Emma.

Meg grinned. "You see your wife as more than just a breeder."

He raised an eyebrow. "Do you read minds as well as dreams?"

She shook her head. "I'm merely observant. What I see between you two is encouraging."

"If you observe a growing friendship, then you're correct."

She crossed the room and pressed her palms

against the candle-laden table that hugged the wall. "Friendship is a safe word."

He stared at her back. "You prefer another?"

She turned to face him. "Love."

His chest tightened. "That word has no meaning for me."

"It could."

"No, it could not."

"You seem very determined, but I wonder if I believe you."

"Why wonder if the path is clear when there's nothing else to travel?"

Slowly, she walked toward him...with presence and purpose. She halted not two feet away. "Of whose path do you speak? Yours or Emma's?"

His gaze locked with hers. "Does it matter? They are one now."

"Exactly," Meg said with a nod. Her violet eyes smoldered. "But know this: if you don't help her break the curse, no one will."

Chapter Seventeen

Emma sighed as she strode across the sunlit bailey. The crisp, fresh air was a welcome change from the thick aromas which clung to her workshop's walls.

True to her word, Gertrude had helped restock the herbs and even now finished cleanup. A twinge of guilt seized Emma as she thought of her cousin standing alone, sweeping the floor of the workshop, but the bright sun melted the feeling away.

Anxious to find William, she hurried up the stairs and into the keep. As she approached the great hall, the sound of his voice arrested her and she peered inside.

He sat in his large, oak chair and held conference with John, the steward. Tall, thin, and mostly bald, the older man stood before William and nodded.

"Sizeable crops have been harvested in all of your manors," John said. "But there's still the matter of the wine in your cellar at Druid's Head."

"Can you sell it?" William asked.

"I'm making inquiries," John replied. "That reminds me, Father Cedric has spoken with the almoner about the food for the poor."

"And the cloth?"

"On its way. One hundred ells, just as you requested."

"Good. It must be here by Michaelmas."

"Consider it done."

William gave John an approving nod. "You're a competent steward."

John bobbed his head. "Thank you, my lord."

Emma stepped out of the shadows. "Indeed," she said in a voice that projected to the corners of the hall. "John is a treasure."

The steward turned, and William stood. Emma fought to keep her attention on John as she approached the two men.

"My lady," said John. "You are too kind."

She shook her head. "Not at all. How is your wife's cough?"

John smiled. "Almost gone, thank you."

"I'm glad to hear it," Emma said. Then she turned to William.

Her heart fluttered as his dark, hot gaze devoured her. Willing herself to remain calm, she asked, "Have you concluded your business, or shall I return later?"

William stepped down from the dais and looked at the steward. "Anything else?"

"Not at the moment," said John. "If you'll excuse me, I have a meeting with the butler and pantler."

William nodded his assent, and John hastened from the hall. Emma stared at William's full lips and remembered where they'd been the night before. Her face burned. With a silent curse, she forced her gaze to his black tunic, but she knew what lay beneath it. Visions of his naked body inundated her mind.

He drew nearer by the second. "Ah," he said. "You look good in pink."

She locked her gaze onto his shining, black eyes. "I'm wearing blue."

"I meant your face."

She couldn't help but smile. "Oh. I blush too easily these days."

He stopped barely a foot away and grinned. "Am I responsible for that?"

"You know you are, but I'm not here to discuss my complexion. I want to show you something."

His smile now boasted teeth. "You showed me plenty last night, but I'm eager for more."

She gave him a pointed look. "I only wondered if you'd seen our bolt-hole."

His eyes widened. "I haven't, and John never mentioned it."

"I'm sure he would've sooner or later, but if you'd like, I'll show you now."

"Where is it?"

"In the storeroom below the solar. Surely John gave you my father's key to the trapdoor."

"He did."

"Do you have it with you?"

William reached inside the leather pouch that hung from his belt. Then he laid the key in her palm. "Lead on, my lady."

They left the hall and passed under the tall, painted arch above the solar's entrance.

"If you'll grab a torch from the stairwell, I'll get the door," Emma said, and she hurried to the far side of the chamber. She knelt beside the rush mat which hid the trapdoor and pushed it aside. At the sound of William's approach, she turned the key in the lock and pulled the door upward.

"I would've opened that for you," he said.

"Thank you," she said, standing, "but I've done it hundreds of times."

"To count riches or utilize the bolt-hole?"

She turned to him. "What do you think?"

"I'd wager you value freedom above wealth."

She handed him the key. "'Tis a wager you'd win."

He passed her the lighted torch. "You first."

Torch in hand, she started down the narrow wooden stairs. William followed and maneuvered the rush mat over the trapdoor.

"No one will know where we've gone," he said, his tone conspiratorial.

Her stomach quivered as the door thudded shut. Why was he so keen to cover their tracks?

Stop it, she scolded herself. *All is well.*

The cellar floor felt firm beneath her feet. She sought one of the iron holders in the chill, stone wall and lowered the torch into it. Light washed over the table, chests, and barrels with detachment, but it seemed to caress her grandmother's tapestry.

At the foot of the stairs, William paused and stared.

"You look spellbound," she said. "Is it the picture or the skill?"

He moved closer to the wall hanging. "Both, I imagine."

"Well, believe it or not, you're actually staring at the bolt-hole."

He looked at her. "What do you mean?"

She pulled the tapestry away from the wall and slid behind it. The next instant, he was beside her, warm and ever so close.

Feeling her way in the darkness, she inched along the wall until her fingers touched wood. Then she raised the bolt and opened the small door. Cold, dank air filled her nostrils, but daylight beckoned at the end of the tunnel.

"You'll have to duck," she said, stepping through the doorway.

"I see what you mean," he said, following her lead.

She closed the door behind them and started toward the light. "Come. The sooner we get out of here, the happier you'll be."

"Who says I'm unhappy?"

Tiny rustles and squeaks brought the passage to life, and she shuddered. "Well, if you're not, I am. Make haste."

When they finally emerged into the thicket, she took a deep breath and turned to him. "Better?"

"Better," he acknowledged with a grin.

"This way," she said.

She led him quickly through the dense shrubbery, then slowed as they reached the orchard. Long rows of apple, pear, plum, and walnut trees dominated the landscape. In the distance, a group of servants picked apples, so she headed in the opposite direction. Quiet and seemingly relaxed, William strolled beside her.

After a short while, she lifted a hand to the lowest branches and kept walking. The leaves tickled her fingers, and she sighed.

William chuckled. "Enjoying yourself?"

"As a matter of fact, I am," she replied. Her smile broadened as a trio of ravens flew overhead.

"*Hremmas*," said William.

She looked at him sharply. "Aye. Ravens. You remembered."

"I told you. I like languages. Besides, I could hardly forget a word so similar to your name."

"But I only said it once."

"The day we met."

"Your pronunciation is remarkable. You've quite an ear for the Saxon tongue."

He shrugged. "Teach me more."

"What would you like to learn?"

"Anything. How about the word for 'tree'?"

She grinned. "*Treow*."

"Sheep?"

"*Sceap*."

"Battle."

"*Orlege*."

"Stallion."

"*Steda* or *stodhors*."

"Breeches."

"*Waedbrec*."

"Desire."

"*Lust*."

"Paradise."

"*Neorxenawang*."

He halted, and she stopped alongside him.

"You're joking," he said.

"Not in the least. And I see right through your choice of words."

He arched an eyebrow. "Oh?"

She made a face. "Try this word, if you will. *Ricceter*."

"What does that mean?"

"Arrogance."

He laughed. "'Tis a good word."

She loved the sound of his laughter. She loved his voice, period.

"Tell me," she said, "why are you so interested in languages?"

He thought for a moment. "Do you remember what you said about fruit? That you love texture as well as taste?"

"Aye."

"Languages are similar. The cultures behind them are like a variety of fascinating flavors, but the words themselves feel good on my tongue. Particularly the more foreign sounds."

"Do you have a favorite language?"

"The Saxon tongue intrigues me at present."

"What of your travels to the Holy Land? Did you like Turkish?"

"I liked Arabic better. The characters are completely different from ours. They're even written in the opposite direction."

"From right to left? That does sound interesting. Could you teach me to write Arabic? My name, perhaps?"

He smiled. "I could," he said. Then his grin turned sly. With predatory grace, he inched toward her. "On one condition."

Her heart tripped. "Which is?"

"You give me another taste of your sweetmeat."

****

Color flooded her cheeks. "Your condition is even more shocking than your language skills."

He looked her straight in the eye. "It shouldn't be. I use my tongue for both."

She gaped at him, and the sight of her ripe, open mouth was his undoing. He pulled her to him and thrust his tongue into her warm sweetness. She returned the kiss at once and pressed her hips against him.

His senses reeled. With a low moan, he tore his lips

197

from hers.

"Unless you want to fulfill my request here and now, I suggest we go inside," he rasped.

Her eyes sparkled. "Through the bolt-hole?"

"Aye."

He grabbed her hand and led her back through the orchard to the twisting thicket. They exchanged the brilliant sun for the cool, black tunnel and tramped blindly onward. To William, the dank passage seemed a mile long.

At last, Emma paused and squeezed his hand. "We're here," she announced, opening the small door.

The next instant, they were both inside, enclosed between the portal and the tapestry. Faint torchlight stole behind the hanging and illuminated Emma's alluring figure.

"Make sure you bolt it," she said, her back to him.

As he lowered the bolt, his patience snapped. He seized her hips and pulled her back against his erection. Lifting her veil, he kissed her nape.

"I'll never get enough of you," he said against her skin.

"You'd get more if we had enough room to move," she replied.

He laughed and squeezed the ample flesh on her hips. "Then hurry. I'm starved for you."

He clung to her as they slid along the wall. Once they emerged into the relative brightness of the storeroom, she started toward the stairs.

"I hope our bedchamber is empty," she said.

From behind, he locked his arms around her waist. "Why?" he said, nuzzling her neck. "We need no bed."

Her body went rigid. "What then?"

"For most meals, a table will suffice."

She glanced at the table in the corner of the room. "You're not serious."

He turned her to face him. "Never more so."

She backed away from him, but he didn't object. With each step, she drew closer to the table.

"What if someone comes?" she asked.

He advanced toward her. "The trapdoor squeaks. I'd hear it, and I'd stop."

Her backside connected with the table's edge. "You'd have to be quick about it."

"Emma, what do the people call me?"

She blinked. "The Storm."

Grasping her waist, he hoisted her onto the table. "I didn't earn the title by dawdling."

He slid his hands under her tunic. Beneath the stockings, her calves were warm and supple. "Lie back," he ordered.

She frowned. "Will—"

He interrupted her with a tender kiss. "Relax," he murmured. He pulled back and eyed her mouth. Her lips were full and flush. Slowly, he met her gaze.

Her eyes claimed him. There was strength and surrender in their violet depths.

"As you wish," she said softly. Then she lay back on the table.

He groaned and shoved aside the layers of linen that separated him from his objective. His heart raced at the sight of her bare, white thighs and the dark triangle between them. Hot blood flowed into his already engorged manhood. In one quick motion, he spread her legs and buried his tongue in her sweetness.

Her gasp was musical, seductive. Her scent was

like perfume; her taste, sublime. He explored her moist, silken folds, and they became his world. He couldn't get enough, couldn't give enough. His tongue found the bud of her desire and caressed it over and over. Slowly, he pushed his index finger an inch into her hot, wet channel. Her moan was his reward.

He was gentle, yet persistent, quickening the motion of his tongue and finger until she writhed on the table. She clutched at the stone wall behind her. Then she grabbed his hair and thrust her hips upward. Suddenly, she cried out. Her tiny passage grew tighter, clenching his fingertip again and again as spasms rocked her core.

He grinned. Then he continued the dual caress of his tongue and finger.

She tried to sit up. "What are you doing?" she panted. "I already felt the release."

"Trust me," he murmured.

With his free hand, he urged her onto her back again. Soon she squirmed anew. Her breaths came in short, shallow gasps.

"No," she moaned. "'Tis too much."

Persistence personified, he continued.

"William," she whimpered. "I shall die!"

He kept her pinned to the table as he intensified the pleasurable assault. With a sudden buck of her hips, she cried out in a pitch higher than before. He paused only to smile, then went back to work.

"What?" she said. "You jest."

"One more," he growled, determined.

Her head tossed on the table. Her hips thrashed. Her fingers tugged on his hair. Again, she climaxed, but this time she shouted his name.

His pride swelled. So did his manhood. With reluctance, he lifted his mouth from her damp, raven curls.

She started to move, then seemed to give up. He stared in awe. With her flushed cheeks and glistening skin, she was beautiful beyond belief. A glowing nymph, awakening to her inherent nature.

He clasped her arms and helped her sit up. She gave him a shy smile. Then she pouted her lower lip and blew cool air at a ribbon of hair that clung to her forehead.

"I had no idea," she said.

He tapped the tip of her nose with his finger. "About what, my raven?"

"That it could happen three times."

"It could've happened more."

Her eyes widened. "Truly?"

He nodded. "With someone as passionate as you, aye."

"Your skill must have something to do with it."

"It does, but you open the door."

Her grin was almost wicked. "Had I known, I might've opened it sooner."

He chuckled and gave her a brief kiss.

"I can smell myself on your lips," she said.

He ran his fingers along the satiny skin of her jaw. "Does that bother you?"

"No. 'Tis unusual, though."

"*You* are unusual. And exotic."

She smiled. "I am?"

He gazed into her violet eyes. 'Twould be so easy to lose himself within them. "You should never doubt it."

"Still, I feel guilty."

"For experiencing pleasure?"

"For not sharing it."

His body ached for her touch. "Do you want to pleasure me?"

She ran her hand along the bulge straining beneath his tunic and breeches. "I do."

Her clothing was still twisted up and around her bare hips. He imagined spreading her legs and thrusting his swollen flesh into her. But he squeezed his eyes shut and fought for control.

"William?" she said uncertainly.

He opened his eyes. "Here," he said. He lifted his tunic with one hand and untied his breeches with the other.

Her fingers closed around him, and he gasped. She was so warm, so willing.

"Shall I stroke you as I did last night?" she asked.

His head fell back. "I'll die if you don't."

Slowly, she began her caress. "Your skin is on fire."

He didn't doubt it, but he could barely think, let alone reply.

"You're so hard and smooth," she continued. "And long."

Excitement raged in his blood. She stroked him harder, faster.

All around stood chests and barrels filled with the symbols of wealth, yet his entire being focused on Emma. The scent of her passion lingered in the air. Her taste still teased his tongue. Her touch, her presence, blazed brighter than the torch on the wall.

Only once before had he come so close to losing

control. In a faraway land where a part of him wandered still.

A surge of sensation rocked his body, and he shut his eyes against the torrent of emotion that lashed his soul. Inexorably and in every sense of the word, Emma unleashed a storm.

Chapter Eighteen

Emma stared down at the parchment on the table and admired the line of squiggles and dots which spelled her name in Arabic. A zealous fire warmed the bedchamber, but 'twas hardly necessary. William's body was an abundant source of heat, and he stood so close she'd begun to perspire.

Setting her quill on the table, she looked up at him. "How's that?"

"Very good," he said, nodding. "I'm impressed."

His approval warmed her even more. With a bright smile, she turned to Tilda, who was whispering to the towheaded manservant at the other side of the chamber. The two looked quite intimate, exchanging grins as they cleared away the remains of supper.

"Tilda," said Emma, "what's so amusing?"

The handmaiden looked up from the platter in her hands, and her brown eyes twinkled. "Nothing, my lady."

Emma couldn't help but return Tilda's smile, though she speculated about its cause.

"I've turned down the bed," Tilda said.

"Thank you," Emma replied.

Tilda glanced at William, then back at Emma. "The pitcher of wine is half-full," she said. "Shall I leave it here?"

"Aye," said Emma.

Tilda nodded. "Do you require anything else?"

Emma turned to William. His eyes held warmth and admiration.

"Do we?" she asked him.

He held her gaze for a long moment, then turned to the handmaiden. "That will be all."

Tilda lowered her eyes and followed the manservant from the room. The sound of their footsteps on the stairs diminished as William strode to the door. He lowered the bolt in place, then grabbed the pitcher of spiced wine from the table.

"Are you thirsty?" he asked.

"No," said Emma.

He poured himself a cup. His large, strong hand dwarfed the vessel.

For what seemed the hundredth time that night, her heart fluttered. Conversation was the only remedy.

"I think the servants are beginning to talk," she said.

He started toward her. "About?"

"We're developing a habit of taking supper in our bedchamber."

"We are indeed. Does that bother you?"

"The habit or the talk?"

"Either."

"Neither one bothers me. You?"

He sipped his wine. "Let them talk. As for the other, what better way to sup than in the solace of this chamber, with you all to myself."

Heat filled her cheeks. She turned swiftly to the parchment. "This writing is fascinating."

Back at her side, William set his cup on the small table. "So are the people who devised it," he said.

"Most of my men saw them as infidels, but a handful of us appreciated their culture. Their apothecaries offer cures for most any illness, and their knowledge of the stars is incredible. The craftsmen are masters of enamel work, and the food...ah! The food contains spices the like of which you've never tasted."

As he spoke, she studied him. His eyes were alight, and his enthusiasm bordered on childlike. When he talked of languages and cultures, he seemed a different man, one who might overcome the world's blackest horrors.

A glimmer of faith stirred within her. She began to hope, as she'd never done before, that he might be capable of love.

"Delectable breads," he continued. "Sauces that bite the tongue."

She beamed at him. "You're making my mouth water."

"No," he said, his gaze suddenly intense. "That's what you're doing to me."

Her heart hammered in her chest. "Oh?"

He sighed. "The parchment has grown tiresome. I need to write on something else. Doff your clothes."

Speechless, she stared at him.

"Go on," he said. "Take them off."

She stepped backward and found her voice. "You would write on my clothing?"

"Guess again."

"Not my skin!"

"Why not?"

"With ink?"

He shook his head. "Something better."

She looked askance at him. "If I must undress, so

must you."

His grin was unnerving. "Now that's a demand worth hearing."

She began to undress. "Well, if you like it so much, get on with it. Strip."

He bowed theatrically. "Your wish is my command."

From beneath a flurry of blue linen, she heard his empty boots hit the floor. By the time she freed herself of her tunics and smock, he was stepping out of his braies.

Her breath caught in her throat. Framed by the glowing hearth, he was a miracle of masculinity, a masterpiece of finely honed muscles, angry scars, and jet black hair. Impressive as his swollen manhood was, 'twas nothing compared to his eyes. She would never tire of them, never wake again without wanting them to revere her body as they did now.

He walked toward her. "You take my breath away," he whispered.

And you may have taken my heart, she thought.

"Come," he said, seizing her hand. "Stand by the fire."

He positioned her between the table and hearth so the blaze warmed her back and buttocks. Grinning, he dipped his index finger into the cup of wine. Then with starts, stops, and squiggles, he moved the wet finger from her shoulder to the base of her neck, right to left, inscribing something on her collarbone.

"What are you writing?" she asked.

"My name, in Arabic," he said.

He bent over the script and, as though writing with his tongue, he licked the wine from her skin. His tongue was hot and extremely dexterous.

She cleared her throat. "You're quite the scribe."

He raised his head. "One must always blot ink so it won't run."

"True, but you're not blotting the wine. You're tracing it. I believe your tongue could paint a picture, if you so choose."

"Why should I paint a pretty picture when I can taste one?"

Again, he dipped his finger into the wine, but this time he knelt before her. With leisurely strokes, he wrote on her abdomen. Then he licked the second word away.

"Those strokes felt similar to the first," she remarked.

"Observant, aren't you?" he said. "I wrote my name again."

"Why just your name?"

He smiled up at her. "I'm marking my territory."

"Is there a need?"

He closed his eyes, bowed his head, and inhaled her unique scent. "There is always a need," he breathed.

The memory of the intense, repeated pleasure he'd given her in the storeroom flooded back to her. She shivered.

"You're cold." He ran his large, warm hands over her hips. "Turn toward the fire."

She wasn't about to reveal the true reason for her trembling, so she obliged him. She gazed into the flames which crackled and leapt in the fireplace. A moment later, William's wet finger flitted across her bottom. "What—"

"Shh," he responded. He clasped her hips and held

her still.

Slowly, his tongue traced the wine on her backside. She shivered anew.

"Still cold," he murmured against the tender flesh.

"That wasn't cold."

"What then? Arousal?"

She rallied her pride. "Indignation, maybe?"

"Why?"

"You wrote your name—"

"On your arse, aye. 'Tis a lovely one too. You have the cutest little dimple on—"

"William!"

"You disliked how it felt?"

"I didn't say that."

"Then there's no reason for me to stop."

"But...you should respect words."

"I respect your arse."

She looked over her shoulder at him. "I'm serious."

His expression was rife with humor. "So am I. The curve of your backside is so perfect that it must have philosophical import."

She sighed. "What I'm trying to say is that words and sounds have power."

"Have they?"

"Aye. So have thoughts. What we think shapes our lives."

He chuckled. "If you only knew what I'm thinking now."

She returned her gaze to the fire. "I'm not sure I want to."

Suddenly, he swept her up in his arms and marched to the bed. Excitement and dread danced within her. His lovemaking was heaven. But there was always the possibility it might go too far.

He laid her on the bed's cool, linen sheets. Then he stretched out beside her. His mouth sought hers, but she caught his face between her hands.

"William," she said.

He frowned. "What is it? You're not afraid—"

"No, but you know my body well. This time, if you'll let me, I want to explore yours."

His brow smoothed. "Of course, my raven." He turned onto his back. "I'm yours for the hunt."

She gave him a shy smile, then ran her fingertips along the rough stubble of his jaw and down his smooth neck. Her gaze dropped to the dark, curly hair spread across his chest. She twisted the strands around her fingers and marveled at their texture; they felt both coarse and soft at once. On impulse, she leaned over and ran her check back and forth over his chest.

"You like that?" he said in an amused tone.

"It feels so nice." She turned her head so the hair tickled her lips and chin. Again, she moved her face across his chest.

"I wonder..." she began. She darted her tongue at his right nipple, then circled it slowly. As her teeth grazed the tender flesh, it hardened. Encouraged, she closed her mouth around the nipple and sucked.

William tensed beneath her and ran his fingers through her hair. He moaned, and she felt a strange sense of power. She sucked the other nipple, then gently bit it.

His response was even louder. She grinned and slid her tongue along the thin line of hair that led to his navel. When she dipped her tongue inside, he laughed.

"Does it tickle?" she asked.

"No," he said, "but it feels good."

She honored the navel with another flick of her tongue, then pulled away to observe his erection. 'Twas huge, and she slid her fingers through the springy hair that framed it. Leaning forward, she moved her cheek over the dark thatch.

"I love the way this feels," she said.

William said nothing. He seemed to be holding his breath.

She moved her cheek along his bulging member to the tight pouch below it. She kissed the sac, then ran her closed lips back up the long, hot shaft. A memory stirred: his mouth on her nether lips; his tongue and the ecstasy it produced. Experimentally, she circled the tip of his manhood with her tongue. Then her mouth sheathed the head of his shaft.

He sprang up and pulled her to him. "Enough," he growled.

In a flash, he rolled her onto her back. His body covered hers. His hands sizzled over her breasts and hips.

He claimed her mouth in a primitive kiss. She groaned and writhed beneath him. His kiss, his touch, even his scent called to her on a primal level she couldn't ignore. She wanted him to ravish her...needed to love him and feel his love in return.

But as his knee parted her legs, a whisper invaded her thoughts.

The curse. Remember the curse!

She could feel his throbbing manhood poised at the threshold of her wet, virginal channel. His breaths were sharp and hot on her ear.

"God, Emma!" he rasped. "I want to fill you up

with sons!"

****

William felt her stiffen beneath him. Through a haze of desire, he regarded her.

"You needn't be afraid," he said. "I'll be as gentle as possible, and you'll feel more pleasure than pain."

She avoided his gaze. "No," she said. "That's not it."

"Is it the curse? Forget it, Emma. We'll prove it wrong."

"You still don't understand."

He rolled off of her and propped himself up with a pillow. "Then you'd better explain."

She moved to sit across from him and hugged her knees to her chest. "All you want is sons."

He frowned. "My desire for heirs is nothing new. I've always made that clear."

With a sigh, she rolled her eyes. "Abundantly so."

He crossed his arms. "So what's the problem?"

She threw up her hands. "All my life, I've lived to please others. I did everything but beg for my father's attention, but he saw me as a disappointment, a nuisance. I've healed the sick and used my visions to warn those in danger. I've tried to be a fair mistress and a dutiful wife. But that's all I am."

"Isn't that enough?"

"Not anymore. I need to be loved for who I am. Not for my medicines or visions, and not because I can give someone castles, land, and children to inherit them. I want to know real love...*your* love."

He had to look away. Her eyes brimmed with pain and longing. He could bear his own, but not hers.

"You cannot ask this of me," he said.

"Why not? Don't I deserve it?"

"You do."

"Then I can hope."

Infernal memories bit into his heart and mind. He had to set Emma straight and lay down the law once and for all. "You mustn't hope for the impossible."

"I'm beginning to believe anything is possible."

"Not in this foul world."

She slammed her palm on the bed. "There's good in it, too."

He shook his head. "You know not whereof you speak."

"I know you've suffered."

"I don't wish to discuss it."

She glowered at him. "Of course not. You'd rather let the pain fester in your soul until there's no room for anything else. Least of all love."

He gritted his teeth. "I banished love long ago."

"Or maybe you've kept it carefully preserved. Is it Sahar you love?"

"Robert should never have told you about her."

"Must I battle a ghost for your affections?"

Heat and adrenaline coursed through him. He leapt from the bed and stamped across the chamber. In silence, he snatched his clothing from the floor and began to dress.

Emma still huddled on the bed. "Answer me," she said. "Do you love her?"

He threw his black tunic over his head. "Don't be absurd," he snapped.

"Shall I take that as a 'no'?"

He whisked his leather belt around his waist. "You can take it any way you like."

"Why won't you talk to me? What's the big secret?"

"My secrets are my own."

"A fine remark, especially after you demanded to know how I felt about Wulfstan."

He shoved his feet into his boots. "That was different. He was very much present."

"Sahar might as well be. But keep your secrets, if they give you such pleasure. Perhaps I have a few of my own."

He looked sharply at her. She hugged a pillow to cover her nakedness.

"What are you saying?" he asked, striding toward her.

She stared past him to the fire. "Nothing," she said.

He stopped beside the bed and towered over her. "I don't believe you."

She glared up at him. "Well, you should. I conceal even less than you convey, and that's a paltry amount indeed."

"Then why would you speak so?"

"Because I'm mad! You treat me like a stranger."

"Emma—"

"Or at best, a breeder."

"I've never treated you as such."

Tears glistened in her eyes. "You're no different from my father," she murmured.

His heart constricted. "You're wrong, Emma."

"Am I?"

He sighed. "How can I convince you?"

Her mouth quivered. "You can love me."

His chest tightened as he stared down at her. "I would gladly give you any of my possessions," he said.

"But love is not among them."

She blinked, and tears rolled down her cheeks. "Then we are truly cursed."

She buried her head in the pillow and began to weep.

William reached out to her, but he withdrew his hand at the last second. Her sobs racked his soul. He couldn't stay. He needed air. With a heavy heart, he grabbed his mantle, trudged to the door, and left the chamber.

Chapter Nineteen

Hours later, Emma woke from a fitful slumber. She rubbed her eyes, rolled over, and peered through the dimness to the hearth. A pile of glowing embers was all that remained of the fire that had burned within. Beyond the castle walls, the night wind sighed. Inside, the chamber seemed as still and lifeless as a tomb.

William had not returned.

Seized by the memory of their argument, she cringed. She'd actually compared him to her father. No wonder he'd needed space.

A disquieting image of the Saracen woman, Sahar, flashed through her mind: a dark-haired, dark-eyed goddess of perfection with whom she could never compete.

God rot her for stealing his heart, she thought, *for inspiring in him what I cannot.*

Her stomach churned. If her husband was free to leave the bedchamber, so was she. She'd use the bolt-hole and go to Woden's Circle, but not for a vision. For strength and calm. To feel her mother's presence.

She tossed the covers aside and jumped out of bed. She dressed quickly, then marched to the largest chest against the wall. Kneeling, she threw open the lid and reached past layers of smooth linen to the back corner, where she hid the storeroom key.

'Twas gone. Frowning, she slid her hand between

the garments and along the oaken sides and bottom of the chest. She found nothing.

Slowly, she stood up. Did William take the key? If so, how did he know where she kept it? Was he trying to protect her, or control her?

At any rate, Woden's Circle was out of the question. She'd never make it past the gatehouse with William's garrison on the watch. She'd have to stay within the curtain wall.

With a sigh of resignation, she grabbed her gray mantle. She slung it over her shoulders and headed for the door.

Down the spiral steps she flew. At the bottom, she spotted an empty wall socket and paused. The torch was missing. She looked toward the solar's entrance. 'Twas dark within, so she started toward the hall.

A creaking sound in the solar stopped her cold. She listened intently. Then she scooted along the wall and peeked inside. A sliver of light on the floor expanded as the trapdoor slowly opened.

She held her breath. The head of a torch, then its full length, emerged. A feminine hand clasped the base, and the woman's identity was soon apparent. 'Twas Gertrude.

Phew, Emma thought. She folded her arms and waited in silence.

Gertrude closed and locked the trapdoor. Then she dragged the rush mat back in place and straightened.

"What have you been up to?" Emma questioned.

Gertrude jumped, and the torch's flame wavered. "Emma?"

Emma stepped into the torchlight's sphere. "As you see," she said.

Gertrude whistled her relief. "You scared the pottage out of me."

"Likewise. Light some candles, will you?"

Gertrude nodded and went to work until a soft glow filled the room. Then she scuttled to the stairwell to replace the torch. When she returned, her expression was guarded.

"Well?" said Emma.

"Well what?"

Emma held out her hand, palm up. "You have my key."

Gertrude lumbered forward and dropped it into Emma's palm. Cold clung to the key.

"Did the storeroom entice you or the bolt-hole?" Emma asked.

"The bolt-hole," Gertrude answered. "Your husband's men guard the gate so closely at night there's no other way out."

"You're right about that."

"And there was one man in particular I wished to avoid."

"Whom?"

Gertrude's eyes narrowed. "Let's just say a member of the garrison has designs on me."

"Designs?"

"Carnal ones."

Emma tilted her head. "Is this the lover you mentioned? The man who hurt you?"

Gertrude looked down and smoothed her dark tunic with meticulous care. "I'd rather not discuss it."

"If you were raped—"

"I was not. I was deflowered but not unwillingly. 'Twas just...not what I expected. Perhaps, if you bedded with Lord Ravenwood, you'd have an easier time of it."

Emma was sure she would, but her immediate concern was for Gertrude. "Is there any way I can help?" She stepped forward.

Gertrude met her gaze. "No. But I feel much better after my walk in the fresh air."

"Wither did you go?"

"Woden's Circle, believe it or not."

"You? Whatever for?"

Gertrude shrugged. "You've preached so often about the peace and beauty there, I decided to give it a try."

"And?"

"'Tis more agreeable than I remembered," Gertrude replied. Then she eyed Emma's mantle. "You're dressed warmly. Wither were *you* going?"

"The same place as you, but I've changed my mind. I shall visit the chapel instead."

"Have you the urge to pray?"

Emma shook her head. "Only the need for reflection. All of Ravenwood will be stirring soon, but the chapel should be quiet."

"'Tis just as well you're staying indoors."

Emma removed her mantle and folded it over her arm. "Why?"

A faraway look arrested Gertrude's features. She brushed past Emma, then halted in front of the window. She spoke without turning. "A storm is brewing."

****

The brisk wind lashed William's cheeks as he emerged from the stairwell and stamped onto the twilit battlements. All night he'd paced: round the bailey, through the darkened keep, and high above it all. Anywhere served, so long as 'twasn't his bedchamber.

As the hours waxed, so did his temper. His mind discharged a clear and terrible record of his life, from the moment he left for the Holy Land to the memory of Emma's tears. He went over the details again and again, stewing in a burst of negativity which was all-consuming.

Now, on the battlements, his mood so blinded him he nearly slammed into the figure approaching from his right. At the last second, he stepped aside. Then he jerked to a halt in recognition.

"Enjoying an early morning stroll?" Robert teased.

"Leave me be," William snapped.

"A fit of bird-watching, perhaps?"

"I want to be alone."

Robert sighed. "Why are you not curled in bed with your wife?"

"Are you deaf, Robert?"

"Only to your dismissals."

William grumbled and stalked to the stone wall. He leaned against its cold, hard strength and peered through the gap between two merlons. A swarm of dark, dense clouds approached Ravenwood and muffled the rising sun.

Out of the corner of his eye, he glimpsed Robert coming up beside him. "I said—"

"Save your commands for someone who'll listen to them," Robert cut in. "I have news, and I think you'll want to hear it."

William turned to him. "What news?"

"In the night, one of your men spotted a lone rider beyond the fields."

"Which man?"

"Erik."

"Whence came the rider?"

"He rode out of the Long Wood and headed north."

"North. To Nihtscua?"

"'Tis possible, but we'll have more information once Erik returns. He followed the rider."

"Good. He's always been one of my best spies."

"The best, I'd say."

"Why was I not told of this?"

"I'm telling you now."

"You know my meaning."

Robert held up his hand, beseeching his brother to wait. Then he yawned loudly.

William's frown deepened. "Don't test my patience, Robert. You'll find it wanting."

"How refreshing."

"Answer my question."

"Your roving about the bailey didn't go unnoticed, and your moods make the men uneasy. Can you blame them for keeping their distance? Besides, Guy said your whereabouts were unknown when it occurred."

William searched his memory. "That must've been when I was in the prison tower."

"Not again."

William glowered at him.

"What did you do there?" Robert questioned.

"I paced...and pondered."

"Brooded, you mean. Ever since our arrival, you've spent a perverse amount of time in that cursed place."

"What if I have?"

"Don't you see it points to a more serious

imprisonment?"

"Of what, pray?"

"Your mind, and I dare say your heart."

"Robert—"

"That's why you're tramping about the cold battlements, instead of enjoying your warm bed."

William turned his back and stared at the storm clouds that swirled ever closer. "I know that," he muttered.

Robert's sigh mingled with the wind's. "If you relish your prison so much, why should you object to my mentioning it?"

William spun around. "You're a fine one to preach! I've not seen you drop to your knees to renew your faith in God and the Holy Church."

"And you never shall."

"Then why pressure me?"

"You're married, Brother. You have more than your own needs to consider."

"Lady Ravenwood wants what I cannot give."

Robert raised an eyebrow. "And that is?"

"Love," William said, as though naming a disease.

"She wants what is her due."

"Because I slid a wedding band onto her finger?"

"No. Because of what she's given you."

"She won't give me an heir. That much I know."

"Well, you'd better listen to what I know. You're happier at Ravenwood than I've seen you in years."

The memory of Emma's violet eyes and spirited smile raided William's thoughts. "'Tis fleeting, Robert. Mere moments of happiness."

"A lifetime can be built from such moments…if you allow it."

Footsteps sounded in the stairwell. Together, the brothers turned as their squires appeared.

Geoffrey seemed to analyze William's stance and expression. "Do you require anything, my lord?"

"Not at the moment," William replied.

Guy turned to Robert. "Have you told him about Erik?"

"Aye," said Robert.

William rubbed his jaw. "'Tis curious the rider should spring from the Long Wood."

Geoffrey frowned. "The same place where your attacker hid."

Guy folded his arms. "Whoever the man is, he must know the forest extremely well to venture into it at night."

Robert nodded. "Why would he risk being seen by our men? What errand is so pressing?"

"An evil one," William answered.

Robert and the squires turned to William as one.

"What do you suspect?" Robert asked.

"I hardly know," William replied, "but I sense trouble."

The far-off sound of a horse's gallop drew them all to the crenellated wall. They strained their eyes to pierce the unusual darkness of the dawn. On the horizon, a lone rider appeared, tearing down from the north.

"Is it Erik?" said Guy.

"I cannot tell," Robert responded.

The rider advanced. His speed spelled peril, urgency. His hair was straight and blond.

"Who is it?" Guy asked.

"Not Erik," Geoffrey said.

A prickle of recognition ran along William's spine.

Robert frowned. "It looks like—"

"Wulfstan," William finished.

"What the devil is he doing here?" Robert said.

William's blood raged in his veins. "What indeed?"

Geoffrey turned to William. "Do you think he was the mysterious rider?"

"Who can say?" William replied.

"He's in quite a hurry," Guy said.

"He would be," Robert murmured, "if Erik's chasing him."

William scanned the quiet hills and dales to the north. "There's no sign of Erik. Not yet." He hastened to the south wall, and the others followed.

Below, Wulfstan slowed his mount as he neared the moat. A whir of excited voices rose from the gatehouse.

Robert regarded William. "Will you receive him?"

"In due course," said William. "But not right away. You must greet him in my stead."

"I?" said Robert.

William lowered his voice. "If Wulfstan was the rider in question, Erik will be along soon. I'll hear my spy's report before I give audience to anyone else."

Robert nodded. "Guy, go to the gatehouse and tell the men to lower the drawbridge," he ordered. "I'll be there anon."

"Aye, sir." Guy spun on his heel and disappeared down the stairs.

Robert turned to William. "What shall I tell our guest?"

William shrugged. "Whatever you like."

"You're asking me to lie."

"I'm telling you to be creative."

Robert gave him a conspiratorial grin. "I'll do my best."

"I don't doubt it," William replied. "Tell the men to be vigilant."

"Understood," said Robert. Then he hurried down the stairs.

William turned to his squire. "And what think you, Geoffrey?"

Geoffrey's eyes narrowed. "Wulfstan's sudden arrival is suspicious."

William nodded. "'Tis why you must help me dress."

The grating of gears sounded below as the portcullis awoke.

"Dress, my lord?" said Geoffrey. "For what?"

"For battle."

Chapter Twenty

Alone in the chapel, Emma shuffled toward the altar. She paused and stared up at the stained glass window. The dim light trickling through it muted the colors. The gold cross on the altar looked just as dull.

With a sigh, she closed her eyes.

She could blame any number of things for her mood. The ailing sun. Her lack of sleep. Gertrude's admission. But they were mere excuses.

The heart of the matter was…well, her heart.

She loved William. How and when the emotion took hold was a mystery, but 'twas undeniable. So was his rigidity.

There was a difference between fearing a thing and feeling it. Hope was possible when she only imagined his emotional limitations. Now that he'd declared them, she was lost.

"Emma?" a familiar voice echoed off the stone walls.

Doubting her ears, she spun around. Wulfstan stood in the chapel doorway.

"May I join you?" he asked.

"Of course," she said. "You're the last person I expected to see. How did you find me?"

He removed his blue, woolen mantle and slung it over his arm as he approached her. "Tilda told me you were here."

"But who told her?"

"Gertrude."

Emma sat on the front bench. "Please, sit."

Wulfstan draped his mantle on a neighboring bench, then joined her. "'Tis good to see you again."

"And you. But why are you here?"

He bounced his knee. "To talk to your husband, but he's unavailable at the moment."

"'Tis early yet."

"Early enough for me to wonder why you're up and about."

She rolled her eyes. "I barely slept."

He nodded. "I thought as much from the dark smudges under your eyes."

"Your honesty does you credit, but 'tis not very flattering. As I recall, you made a similar comment the day after my wedding."

"I did, and it worries me. You must look after your health. If Lord Ravenwood—"

"I love him." She folded her hands as though praying.

Wulfstan's ice blue eyes widened, then stared into hers. "I believe you do."

Her shoulders slumped as fatigue washed over her. "But he doesn't love me."

"Has he said so?"

"Aye. What's worse, he says he never will."

"Never is a strong word."

Her gaze fell to her lap. "I know something stronger. His love for another."

"He's taken a mistress?"

"He may as well have."

"Who is she?"

"A ghost from his past, someone he met in the Holy Land."

"She's not here at Ravenwood, is she?"

"No, and according to Sir Robert, she disappeared long ago."

"What was her name?" There was a sudden edge to his voice.

She looked up at him. "Sahar."

Wulfstan glanced here and there, unseeing, as if his mind pieced together a puzzle. "I think you're wrong about her."

"How would you know?" Emma asked. Then she gasped. "Your vision, the day of the attack!"

He nodded. "I thought it best not to share it then, but it might comfort you now."

Her heart pounded. "Tell me."

"I saw the whole thing through your husband's eyes. 'Twas dark. He entered a cave that glowed with firelight. I could feel his excitement, and then..."

"What?"

"He came upon a naked couple making love beside the fire. The man's back was to him, so his face was hidden. But the woman was clearly Sahar."

"How can you be sure?"

"Lord Ravenwood screamed her name in his mind."

Emma felt numb. "Was it rape?"

Wulfstan shook his head. "That was the worst of it. Sahar noticed Lord Ravenwood and smiled at him, as though she'd expected him to come. Then several men grabbed him from behind, and she started laughing. She and her new lover had plotted his capture."

"Blessed Virgin," Emma whispered.

"The soldiers forced him from the cave, and Lord Ravenwood's emotions exploded. Shock, rage, despair. I felt all of it, just as he did. And there my vision ended."

"If only the experience ended for Lord Ravenwood, but it didn't."

"You know what happened afterward?"

"He became Hattin's prisoner."

"Hattin?"

"A Saracen chief with a taste for torture."

Wulfstan frowned. "I see."

Her heart twisted as she imagined William's pain. "Betrayed by the woman he loved," she said. "Sir Robert never mentioned that."

"I doubt he knows. The memory was so strong and buried so deep. I don't think Lord Ravenwood told a soul."

She bit her lip. "Now I understand. No wonder he cannot love."

"Don't be so sure. Your husband is a powerful man, and if he doesn't love, 'tis because he chooses not to."

"After what he's suffered, how could he choose otherwise?"

"He could start by believing in you."

She shook her head. "Not so easy."

"Perhaps not, but he does care for you in some capacity. He took an arrow for you. And he was jealous of our relationship. With time, and prolonged physical contact, he's bound to love you."

"Physical contact," she muttered.

"Aye," he said. "The act of love is spiritual and binding."

"So if I bedded with him, his heart would become more vulnerable."

"I would expect it. But the curse is still a threat."

A once discarded seed took root in her mind. "What if I found a way around it?"

Wulfstan placed his hand over hers. 'Twas warm, encouraging. "All the better, but I'd still advise you to weigh the risks."

Hope rustled deep within her. "I think I already have."

"But I haven't told you everything about my vision," he said in a hushed voice. "'Tis why I must speak with Lord Ravenwood."

She leaned forward. "What is it?"

Just then, a movement at the chapel entrance caught her eye. Robert lurked in the doorway.

"Cozy, aren't we?" he said, crossing his arms.

She yanked her hands from Wulfstan's grasp and jumped to her feet. Leisurely, Wulfstan rose and grabbed his mantle from the bench.

Robert watched him. "My brother will see you now."

"Good," Wulfstan replied. Then he turned to Emma. "We'll talk later."

"Later," she agreed.

As Wulfstan strode to the door, she glanced at Robert.

"My lady," Robert said, bowing. When he straightened, he grinned.

She smiled back at him. At least he trusted her.

As the men vanished through the archway, she planned her next move. 'Twould work if Wulfstan was right. It had to work, and the end was worth any means.

Suddenly, Gertrude appeared in the doorway. "Well?" she said, hurrying forward. "What said Wulfstan?"

Emma did her best to look casual. "Nothing much. Only that he must speak with Lord Ravenwood."

Gertrude's eyes narrowed. "Then why do you look like you were just crowned queen of all England?"

Emma pushed her shoulders back. "I've made a decision."

"About?"

"My marriage bed. I know you overheard my conversation with Meg in the workshop, so you must know of the drink that prevents pregnancy."

"Are you willing to try it?"

"I am."

Gertrude grinned. "How extraordinary! I came to suggest that very plan and urge you to try it at once. I'm sure when you become Lord Ravenwood's lover, you'll win his heart."

Longing, intense and undiluted, surged through Emma. To lie in William's arms without fear or restraint would be bliss, a dream come true.

For an instant, Gertrude frowned. Then a smile brightened her face. "We must act quickly," she said. "I'll find Meg and have her mix the potion. You go to your chamber and wait for me there. Tell no one what we've planned. If your husband knew, he'd be furious."

Emma nodded. "I want him to sire an heir, just not until I've secured his love."

"Of course," said Gertrude, her green eyes sparkling. She grasped Emma's hand and pulled her toward the door. "Make haste. We've not a moment to spare."

****

William clasped the cool hilt of his sword as he climbed the prison tower's winding staircase. The weight of the chain mail beneath his mantle was familiar and reassuring. So was the knowledge that his men were ready for a fight, if one was needed. Less comforting was Erik's continued absence. Regardless, 'twas time to face Wulfstan.

Robert's deep voice reached William's ears halfway up the stairs. "Do we owe this foul weather to your presence?" Robert asked Wulfstan.

The Saxon's voice was just as resonant. "Strange as it may seem, my moods do affect the elements."

"Fascinating," said Robert. He stood before the dormant fireplace and glanced at the doorway as William crossed the threshold. "Ah, my brother."

With preternatural grace, Wulfstan pivoted on his heel and leveled his bright blue gaze on William. "Lord Ravenwood," he said with a nod.

William challenged Wulfstan's stare with his own. "Let's say I believe in your link to the weather. Why is your mood so dark?"

A shadow fell over Wulfstan's face. "All last night, I sensed something was wrong. Once I realized sleep was hopeless, I came hither to warn you."

"A noble gesture," said William. "But can you be more specific?"

"Unfortunately not," Wulfstan replied. "'Tis but a feeling of disquiet centered on Ravenwood."

William had the same feeling. "I wouldn't have expected your concern for our welfare."

Wulfstan raised an eyebrow. "And I wouldn't have expected us to meet in a prison."

William shrugged. "You told Robert you wished to speak with me in private. This tower seemed the perfect place. But why the need for secrecy?"

Wulfstan glanced over his shoulder at Robert.

Robert raised his hand and performed a casual, impertinent wave. "I'm still here."

"I see that," Wulfstan responded. Then he turned back to William. "Do you wish to hide anything from your brother?"

William exchanged a soulful look with Robert. "No."

"Then I'll continue," said Wulfstan. "I don't know how much your wife has told you of my abilities."

"Do you think we discuss you at every meal?" William snapped.

Wulfstan clenched his hands, then relaxed them. "Hardly."

"You can assume I've heard nothing."

"Then let me inform you. I have the Sight."

"That gift seems commonplace here in the north," William said.

Wulfstan looked relieved. "Then Lady Ravenwood told you about her visions. Mine are different from hers because they stem from personal contact. When I touch people, I see moments from their past. Specifically, what hurt them in the past."

"Why are you telling me this?"

"You may not remember, but I touched you the day you were attacked at Woden's Circle."

William's chain mail felt heavier, constrictive. "Are you implying you had a vision about me?"

"About your past, aye."

"Ridiculous."

"You can judge the truth of my words soon enough."

William shifted his weight from one foot to the other. "Proceed."

"I saw a cave in the Holy Land."

William froze.

"Lovers beside a fire," Wulfstan continued.

"Impossible." William clutched the hilt of his sword.

"You went thither to meet her, but she was with another man."

"Stop!"

Wulfstan raised his chin. "I saw her smile and heard her laugh. She planned your capture…and relished it."

"Not another word," William warned, but his feet seemed glued to the floor.

"Her name was Sahar."

Heat raced along William's nerves. "How dare you speak her name!"

"What?" said Robert.

William ripped his gaze from Wulfstan and regarded his brother.

Robert's gray eyes were wide, disbelieving. "'Tis true?"

"Aye," William said through clenched teeth.

Robert shook his head. "Why didn't you tell me?"

"Whom would it have served?"

"Whom did it serve not to?"

"Me," William growled. "I told you only what I could bear to remember."

"God's teeth!" Robert swore. "How could she betray you? After all you gave her. Filthy, malicious,

Saracen bitch!"

"Too right," said William. "What I told you about her lover was true. I don't know who he was, but I believe he had a hand in my capture."

"So do I," said Wulfstan.

William glared at him. "What are you saying? That you can divine his motive?"

"No," said Wulfstan. "But I know his name."

The power of speech deserted William. He glanced at Robert, who looked equally astonished. Was it possible that after so long a time, they'd finally learn the man's identity?

At last, William found his tongue. "If this is some twisted attempt at humor—"

"I assure you, 'tis not," Wulfstan said.

William folded his arms. "I'm listening."

With knitted brow, Wulfstan turned and stared into the empty hearth. "My vision was clear. I saw everything, including the symbol on the man's arm. A blue serpent."

The long-buried image—which had resurfaced only once, the day Meg described her bizarre dream—dominated William's mind. "Aye," he said. "I remember it."

"'Tis a permanent mark, a pigment fixed into the skin."

"You seem to know a great deal about this serpent."

"I should. I've seen it many times before."

Wulfstan hesitated. Tension stretched the length and breadth of the prison chamber.

"Where?" said William.

Wulfstan turned to him as a rumble of thunder

penetrated the cold, stone walls. "On my brother's arm."

Chapter Twenty-One

Emma paced the bedchamber floor, and each step released the scents of meadowsweet and marjoram from the herb-strewn rushes. Her heart swelled. Her stomach fluttered. Tonight was the night.

A roll of thunder drew her to the open window. She peered out at the darkened fields and the bustling bailey below. A gust of cool wind brushed her cheeks, and she closed her eyes, reveling in the sensation.

The chamber door closed with a thump. She spun around.

"I have it," Gertrude said, hastening forward. She held a small flask in one hand and a pewter cup in the other. "Meg said you must drink it immediately for it to work tonight."

Emma stepped forward. "What's in the cup?"

"Mint water to wash away the taste." Gertrude handed her the flask. "Meg said the medicine would be bitter."

Emma raised the flask to her nose. "I can certainly smell the rue. I wouldn't have guessed so much was necessary."

"Meg assured me she used the proper amount," Gertrude said. "But you'll have to drink all of it."

Emma rolled her eyes. "How did I know you were going to say that?"

"Go on," Gertrude urged.

Tentatively, Emma sipped the medicine. She shuddered as the acrid liquid slid down her throat. "Bitter is hardly the word," she said. "'Tis revolting."

"Drink it quickly," Gertrude advised. "All at once."

Emma nodded and steeled herself against the foul taste. With eyes closed, she gulped down the medicine. Gertrude swiftly reclaimed the flask and thrust the cup into Emma's hands.

Eagerly, Emma drained it. She'd never been so grateful for the taste of mint, but as she swallowed the last drop, she winced. She handed the cup back to Gertrude, then touched her temple. Her head throbbed.

Gertrude appeared anxious, watchful. "What is it?"

Emma rubbed her temple and took a deep breath. "My head."

Gertrude stepped backward. "Perhaps you drank too fast."

Emma stared past Gertrude to the wall beyond. The stones seemed to shift. The surrounding furniture began to sway.

She blinked. "I'm dizzy."

"Of course you are," said Gertrude. Her stance and tone of voice had changed.

Emma searched her cousin's luminous, green eyes. "Did Meg say to expect that?"

"No."

"Then why—"

"Because I poisoned you."

It took a moment for the words to penetrate the fog in Emma's head. Heat flooded her body. Her mouth went dry.

"Poison," she said. "Is it fatal?"

Gertrude smiled. "It had better be."

Her words stung. All at once, Emma remembered her prophetic vision.

If only she'd understood it. If only she could see William once more.

Sorrow, anger, and intense nausea battled for precedence within her. "Why?" she choked.

Gertrude's sneer transformed her face. 'Twas ugly, inhuman. "Because I hate you," she snarled. "All these years, I've bided my time and dreamt of the day I'd be rid of you. I rejoiced in the news of your marriage, because I thought the curse would prevail. But you were stubborn, as always, and refused to allow a man into your bed. If you'd just married Wulfstan like I advised, you would've been under Aldred's control."

Emma felt numb. "Aldred," she murmured.

Gertrude laughed. "Haven't you guessed? What a stupid, simple soul you are. 'Twas Aldred I met last night at Woden's Circle. *He* is my lover...not one of your husband's impotent goblins. Soon we'll be married. Then together, we shall rule Ravenwood."

Emma fought to focus on Gertrude's face, but there were two of them. "Do you expect my husband to cower and run away after my death?"

"No. I expect Aldred to kill him."

Fear clawed at Emma. Her throat constricted. "What right have you to Ravenwood?" she rasped.

Gertrude smirked. "All of your visions, your uncanny eye for detail, and you never suspected. You and I aren't cousins, Emma. We're sisters."

Emma's stomach burned. Her senses reeled. She stumbled to the bed and leaned against it.

"Your father was mine," Gertrude explained.

Emma shook her head, and the chamber spun. "He

bedded his own sister?"

"He knew I was his daughter, just as you knew I was his favorite. Father and I were alike, you see, and I was firstborn. Ravenwood should be mine."

"No. Ravenwood was my mother's birthright."

"The dead have no rights."

"You're mad."

"I'm practical. You'd be dead already if your brute of a husband hadn't jumped in front of Aldred's arrow. But where Aldred failed, I've succeeded."

Emma fell to the floor. The rushes were prickly, blurry. She opened her mouth, but speech was too difficult.

"I can't wait to tell him," Gertrude continued. "He awaits me in the woods."

There was a slight rustle, followed by the sound of Gertrude's footfalls moving farther and farther away. "Fear not, Sister," Gertrude hissed. "You won't be lonely as you rot in your grave. Your precious Norman will soon follow."

The door creaked, then slammed shut. Emma roused her last ounce of strength.

Must stand, she thought, reaching for the bed. *William needs...*

She clung to consciousness, but it slipped away. Her hand and arm flopped to the floor.

****

"Aldred?" said William.

Robert leaned against the prison wall. "I don't believe it."

Wulfstan crossed his arms. "I speak the truth."

William's eyes narrowed. "Or a clever lie."

"Why would I lie?"

"Why would you warn me against your own brother?" William asked.

Wulfstan's arms dropped to his sides. "'Tis the right thing to do. I've wrestled with my conscience long enough."

William glanced at Robert, who shrugged in response. Then he returned his gaze to Wulfstan. "What do you expect me to do with this knowledge?" he asked. "Fight your brother, die by his sword, and leave you a happy widow to wed?"

"I have no desire to wed."

William snorted.

"And your death would not make your wife happy," Wulfstan said.

"You assume a lot."

"I assume nothing. I know."

William stared at him for a long moment. "How do you know?"

Robert stepped forward. "Perhaps they shared confidences in the chapel."

William raised an eyebrow. "The chapel?"

"I found him there with Lady Ravenwood," Robert explained.

William glared at Wulfstan. "Oh?" he said in a low, controlled voice. "What did you there?"

Footfalls echoed in the stairwell. Geoffrey bounded up the last few steps and raced through the doorway. "My lord," he said between rapid breaths. "You must come quickly. 'Tis Lady Ravenwood. She's unwell."

William's chest tightened. "What's wrong with her?"

"We don't know," said Geoffrey. "Tilda found her lying on the floor in your bedchamber. We cannot wake her."

William turned to Wulfstan. "You were the last to see her," he snapped.

Wulfstan shook his head. His eyes were ablaze with emotion. "I'm as shocked as you are."

"If you've hurt my wife—"

"I've not!"

"We'll see about that," William said. He glanced at Robert, then Geoffrey. "Stay here, both of you. Watch him. Under no circumstance is he to leave."

Robert nodded and fixed his gaze on Wulfstan.

"Aye, my lord." Geoffrey darted out of the way.

William dashed past his squire and flew down the stairs. Oblivious to everyone and everything around him, he raced to the bedchamber.

Beyond the open doorway, Emma lay on her back on the floor. Pale. Motionless.

Tilda knelt beside her. She was sobbing, chafing Emma's lifeless hand.

Paralyzed, he held his breath. 'Twas impossible. Unendurable.

Tilda looked up. "My lord!"

He searched her tear-stained face. "Is she alive?"

"Aye, but her breathing is shallow."

Relief coursed through him. Springing into motion, he rushed forward and fell to his knees beside Emma. He gazed down at her ashen face and grabbed her other hand. 'Twas cold. Too cold.

"Have you any idea what happened?" he questioned.

Sniffling, Tilda shook her head. "None."

He glanced at the open window, then gritted his teeth. "Right," he said. "Go and find Meg."

"I cannot leave—"

"Tilda, listen to me like you've never listened to anyone before. You must find Meg. She's our only hope."

Tilda stared at him. Then she gently laid Emma's hand on the floor.

"Aye, my lord." She wiped her eyes. The next instant, she jumped up and rushed out the door.

He scanned the chamber for clues. All was in order. Frowning, he released Emma's hand and lifted her in his arms. He stood and carefully laid her on the bed.

The bedstead groaned as he sat beside her. He pushed a strand of raven hair from her forehead. "Emma," he whispered.

She looked so beautiful, so still. More fragile than he'd ever imagined. If only she'd open her eyes. Move. Moan. Anything would be preferable to the blaring silence that scraped his ears.

He grabbed her hand and willed his strength and warmth into it. But 'twasn't enough. He was powerless to help. All he could do was wait.

Chapter Twenty-Two

An eternity passed before William heard voices in the stairwell. He gazed once more at Emma's ethereal face, squeezed her hand, and stood. Then he turned to the doorway.

With hunched shoulders and bowed head, Meg hobbled into the chamber. Tilda followed behind, pressing her hand to the older woman's back as though for support.

"What happened?" he asked.

Tilda stepped forward and linked her arm through Meg's. "I found her lying on the workshop floor."

Meg lifted her head. Her violet eyes, though dulled by pain, were still as striking as Emma's. "Someone snuck up behind and hit me over the head."

"God's blood!" he swore.

"Or mine," Meg said. She raised a hand to the back of her head and grimaced.

"There were shards of clay on the floor," Tilda said. "Who would do such a thing?"

He advanced and took Meg's free arm. The movement gave her a clear view of Emma's prostrate form. "Holy Mother," she whispered. "This is what Emma saw in her vision. Help me to her."

Together, William and Tilda guided Meg to the bed. Once there, she pushed their hands aside.

"I'm well enough," she said. Leaning forward, she

examined Emma's hands. She lifted Emma's eyelids, checked the inside of her mouth, and sniffed at her lips. Then she straightened. "I suspected as much."

His throat constricted. "What is it?"

"Poison," said Meg.

Tilda gulped. "No!"

He could barely swallow. "Why would she take poison?"

"And what did she take?" said Meg. "I think I smelled rue, but there's something else and 'tis overpowered by mint. Saw you a cup or bottle lying around?"

He shook his head. "Not a one."

She tapped her lip with her forefinger. "Then there's no trace of it. How can I heal her when I don't know what poisoned her?"

A chill ran down his spine, but he ignored it. Now was the time for discipline, logic. "If she were alone when she took it, the container would still be here."

Meg's frown deepened. "Someone must've given it to her, then cleaned up the evidence."

He nodded. "I'll wager 'twas the same person who attacked you in the workshop."

Tilda wrung her hands and looked from William to Meg. "No one at Ravenwood would harm her ladyship," she said. "It had to be an outsider."

"A stranger wouldn't know of Emma's workshop," Meg said. "Nor could he find his way to her bedchamber without someone noticing."

William rubbed his stubbly chin. "Unless he were knowledgeable."

Meg regarded him. "A knowledgeable stranger?"

"There is one among us who fits that description,"

he said.

"Wulfstan," Tilda breathed, her brown eyes wide.

Meg gasped. "Wulfstan is here?"

"He came at daybreak," Tilda said.

Meg's eyes brightened. "Then there's hope."

William scowled. "I fail to see how his presence inspires hope."

Meg clapped her hands together. "'He has the Sight. If he touches Emma, he might see which poison affected her."

"Aye!" said Tilda.

William glanced at Emma. "He will not touch my wife. For all we know, he's the one who poisoned her."

"He would never hurt Emma," Meg said.

"I have no proof of that."

Meg stamped her foot. "No, all you have is your pride. The longer you nurse it, the greater the chance Emma will die!"

"She will not die!" he bellowed. Then he dropped his head and expelled a long breath. "She cannot."

The clop of boots on stone shot up the stairwell and through the open door. Robert's squire hurried into the chamber.

"My lord," Guy said, panting. "You're needed in the bailey."

"Has Erik returned?" William asked.

"No, but we have another visitor," Guy said. Then he noticed Emma on the bed. "My lord, is she—"

"She's still alive," William said.

"For now," Meg added.

The color drained from Guy's face. He crossed himself as a drumroll of thunder sounded outside. "Will you come, my lord?"

"I've no time for visitors," William said.

A sudden spark lit Guy's blue eyes. "You'll have time for this one."

William's skin prickled. "Who is it?"

"Aldred the Merciless."

****

Every black emotion William had ever experienced seethed within him as he strode into the keep's forebuilding. Several of his men lined the walls and watched him in silence. Beyond the stone's protection, thunder rumbled again. 'Twas closer this time. The storm was near.

He stepped through the archway into the open wind. His gaze shot to the gatehouse, where a row of ravens perched. Had they gathered for a show? Or a showdown?

He clutched the hilt of his sword. 'Twas cool, hard. He scanned the faces of his men. Then his eyes narrowed as they focused on the menace in their midst.

In the center of the courtyard, atop his gray stallion, sat Aldred. The howling wind lifted his sapphire cloak so it billowed about him. He, too, wore chain mail...and his sword.

Heat engulfed William. He fought for control as he descended the steps to the bailey floor. With a slow stride, he approached Aldred. He circled the gray warhorse for a full minute, then halted at its side.

"Won't you dismount?" he said coolly.

"I'd rather stay where I am," Aldred said, his tone imperious.

"I'm not surprised," William muttered.

"But you should be. Very surprised. 'Tis not every day one's bride is poisoned."

William's fingers grazed the friendly hilt of his sword. "How do you know that?"

Aldred reeked of conceit. "I arranged it."

William moved fast. His sword hissed as it left its scabbard. He poised the blades's tip against Aldred's neck. "Give me one reason," he grated.

"I'll give you a reason not to. I'm the only one who can save Lady Ravenwood."

Time stood still. So did William, and 'twas the hardest thing he'd ever done.

I could kill him now, he thought. *All who live under the weight of his cruelty would be free...but that wouldn't help Emma.*

He lowered his sword and thrust it back in its scabbard.

"That's better," said Aldred. "Now, I'll make you a deal."

"I don't deal with villains," William said.

"You have no choice. Only two people know what poisoned Lady Ravenwood, and I am one of them."

"Who else knows?"

"The woman who poisoned her. Gertrude."

William went cold. "Her scorn for Normans is brazen," he said. "But why would she hurt her own cousin?"

"She's not Lady Ravenwood's cousin. She's her sister."

William frowned. "Lady Ravenwood never told—"

"She never knew. Gertrude should be mistress here, and she's waited long enough. 'Twas time for action, and a poisoned drink was the next best thing to a poisoned arrow."

William's vision narrowed to a single point:

Aldred's sneer. The Saxon's stained teeth looked like fangs.

"'Twas you," William said in a low voice.

Aldred nodded. His blue eyes gleamed.

"Where is Gertrude?" William snapped.

"Halfway to Nihtscua by now. We met a short while ago, in the woods that separate your lands from mine."

"The North Woods?"

"The very same."

So you were the rider Erik chased, William thought.

Aldred gave him a knowing look. "You needn't hold your breath waiting for your mewling spy to return."

"Mewling?"

"He cried like a woman as he died."

William's body shook. Aldred was vile, venomous. He had to be stopped.

Aldred grinned. "To be fair, he had a right to. His death was slow and painful. I rather enjoyed it."

"You'll pay for this," William said through gritted teeth.

"'Tis you who shall pay...and handsomely, if you ever want to see your wife's lovely, violet eyes again."

"You walking, talking pustule!"

"Call me names if you must, but you should thank me. Gertrude thinks she used sufficient poison to kill Lady Ravenwood at once, but that's not the case. You see, I know something of herbs, so I advised her of the 'correct' amounts. Not too much, not too little. Just enough to keep your wife alive while we strike our deal."

"What deal?"

"'Tis quite simple. I give you the name of the poison. You give me Ravenwood."

William grasped the solid hilt of his sword. "The king would not approve."

"The king cares only for his scholarly books and the purple cushions that warm his arse."

"You've obviously never met him."

"And you've overlooked my generosity. I'll let you keep your other manors."

"Those manors are not yours to give."

"That may be, but the longer we tarry, the faster Lady Ravenwood's life drains from her body."

Dark clouds eddied above. Lightning flashed, and William felt the answering thunder deep within him.

"You really are a serpent," he said.

Aldred's eyes narrowed to blue slits. "Why do you say that?"

"Why do you think?"

"You're referring to the mark on my arm. How—"

"I know, Aldred."

"Know…what exactly?"

"'Twas you who betrayed me to Hattin."

Aldred's features twisted and became more angular. He looked demonic. "You give as good as you get," he said.

"You'd do well to remember that."

"What I remember is Sahar's eagerness to deceive you. How we laughed when Hattin's men dragged you off into the night!"

An unexpected calm washed over William. "I don't doubt it," he said smoothly.

Aldred bristled. "You don't care?"

"I have more pressing concerns," William replied. "Wait here." He turned to leave.

"If this is a trick—"

William cut him off with orders to his garrison. "Raise the drawbridge and close the gate," he said above the rising wind. "Watch him. He doesn't stray from this spot."

"Aye, my lord," a chorus of male voices answered.

He eyed the three knights closest to Aldred. They looked angry, restless.

"Whatever happens, don't take his life," William commanded. "Lady Ravenwood's may depend on it."

Chapter Twenty-Three

William burst into the prison chamber. Robert, Wulfstan, and Geoffrey stared at him in silence. Outside, a thunderclap rippled the morning sky.

"Lady Ravenwood has been poisoned," William announced.

The three men gasped.

"Does she live?" Wulfstan asked.

"Barely," William answered.

Robert stepped forward. "Do you know who poisoned her?"

"Gertrude," William said. Then he turned to Wulfstan. "Under Aldred's direction."

Wulfstan slammed the side of his fist against the stone wall. "I knew something was wrong."

"That's not all," William continued. "Your brother is here."

"Now?" said Wulfstan. "For what purpose? To gloat?"

"You know him well," said William. "But he came to make a deal."

Robert frowned. "What kind of deal?"

"Meg doesn't know what type of poison was used," William explained. "Of course, Aldred does, and he's offered to identify it."

Wulfstan's mouth twisted. "In exchange for what?"

"Ravenwood," William said.

A second collective gasp filled the chamber. Thunder pounded the outer walls of the keep.

"The gall of that man!" Robert exclaimed.

"'Tis more than gall," Wulfstan said. "His soul is diseased."

"He planned it well," Robert remarked.

"That's his forte," said Wulfstan. "He studies his victims, then backs them into a corner until they have no choice but to surrender."

Robert crossed his arms. "My brother does not surrender."

"Then he'd better think fast," said Wulfstan.

Robert regarded him for a long moment. Then he turned to William. "What about your other manors?"

"Aldred said I could keep them," William said. "But I don't believe him for a second."

"As well you shouldn't," Wulfstan said. "He won't stop till he has them all."

William eyed Wulfstan. Perhaps he'd misjudged him. The Saxon's intentions might be just as they appeared: honorable. "Meg thought you might be able to help Lady Ravenwood," he said. "If you could identify the poison she took—"

"We could save her," Wulfstan finished. "I'll do it."

"Good," said William, turning to his squire. "Geoffrey, take him to Lady Ravenwood. Then join the other men in the bailey."

"Aye, my lord," Geoffrey said, squaring his shoulders. With a glance toward Wulfstan, he started for the door.

Wulfstan followed but stopped on the threshold and looked back at William. "What will you do?"

William sighed. His eyes felt dry, scratchy. If only he'd slept the night before.

"I'll stall Aldred and hope for a miracle," he said.

"And if there is none?" Wulfstan pressed.

William stared at the prison's bleak, gray walls, and a tide of emotions surged within him. The wheel of fate was turning faster, closing in on his world.

"Then I must choose," he said, "between Ravenwood and my wife."

****

Lightning streaked the purple sky as William and Robert emerged from the keep. Side by side, they descended to the bailey. The air was electric, and the ground vibrated from the thunder.

All of Ravenwood had congregated in the courtyard. Even the clangs from the smithy had ceased. High above, ravens lined the curtain wall. Ever watchful, they cocked their heads and cawed their secrets to one another.

The people's whispers drifted on the wind, and William intuited their words. *Aldred the Merciless. William the Storm. Will they battle? Who will die?*

Across the bailey, Aldred's stallion reared. Its high-pitched neigh sliced through the wind like a dagger. Aldred curbed the animal, then turned his icy gaze on William.

Robert grumbled. "I wish you could draw your sword and cleave him in twain," he muttered.

William kept his eyes on Aldred. "Patience, Robert," he said. "You may get your wish."

"But what if Wulfstan fails? Will you choose your land or your lady?"

A myriad of images filled William's mind.

Emma's twinkling, violet eyes. Her tender smile. Their first kiss inside the prison chamber. Her droll expression when she made the outrageous comment about well-endowed horses. Her fingers stroking his misshapen finger to soothe his buried pain.

"There never was a choice," he said finally. "I shall not abandon Lady Ravenwood."

Robert's smile was poignant. "If Father were alive, he'd say this, but I hope it means as much coming from me. I'm proud of you."

William turned to his brother, whose gray eyes were the exact shade their father's had been. A rush of emotion warmed his heart and renewed his strength. "Thank you, Robert," he said.

Aldred's razor-sharp voice cut across the bailey. "Have you decided?"

William steeled himself and gave his brother a meaningful look. "Shall we?"

"I wouldn't miss this for the world," Robert replied.

Together, they strode across the courtyard. William raised his face to the network of lightning and thunderclaps that shook the sky. He reveled in the storm. It empowered him.

Aldred snorted as the brothers stopped in front of him. "I see you've brought your bloodhound."

Robert smiled. "How well you put it," he said smoothly. "Your stink drew me hither."

William's mouth twitched. "Will you never come down from your horse?"

"I've no reason to," Aldred retorted.

"Perhaps you're afraid," William said.

Aldred threw him a withering look, and his wh

255

blond hair flailed wildly. "'Tis you who should be afraid!"

"Then dismount," said William.

Aldred glowered at him for a long moment, then swung himself off the warhorse. "Happy?"

"Ecstatic," William replied.

Aldred smirked. "An odd state for one whose wife is slipping away."

Ignoring the gibe, William looked toward the stable. He caught a groom's eye and snapped his fingers. The man scurried forward and led Aldred's horse away.

"Your servants are very alert," Aldred commented. "I shall enjoy their attentions when I am master here."

"I doubt they'd be so attentive to you," Robert said. "They respect Lord Ravenwood."

"Respect," Aldred spat. "Fear is a much stronger incentive."

"Ah," said William. "I've heard of your methods."

Aldred bared his teeth in a feral smile. "Fame suits me. But enough talk. What is your decision?"

All of a sudden, Aldred went rigid. He gaped at something behind William.

William and Robert shared a quick glance. Then they followed Aldred's gaze to the keep's forebuilding. Wulfstan raced down the steps. Like the restless wind, his blue mantle flowed behind him.

The assembled crowd gasped and murmured as Wulfstan strode across the bailey. William and Robert hurried toward him.

So did Aldred. "What are you doing here?" he snarled at his brother.

Wulfstan lifted his chin. "I came to help."

"When did you arrive?"

"Long before you."

"There's no way you overheard my plans."

"You're right," Wulfstan said calmly. "But I sensed them."

Aldred snickered. "How? You possess no true magic."

"You ought not to dismiss my talents, Aldred. They've just defeated you."

Aldred's eyes narrowed. "What do you mean?"

Wulfstan turned to William. "I identified the poison," he said. "Meg knows what to do."

William released a long breath he hadn't been conscious of holding.

Aldred reached for his dagger. "You—"

"Don't!" Robert commanded, his own dagger already poised at Aldred's throat.

Wulfstan grinned at Robert, then shifted his gaze to Aldred. "Well, Brother," he said, "it seems we're all quicker than you."

Robert snatched Aldred's dagger with his free hand, then lowered his own. Aldred's face grew redder by the second.

William regarded Aldred. "Your lever is shattered. You've lost."

"I've lost nothing!" Aldred shouted.

"Look around," Robert said. "'Tis over."

"Not quite," William remarked. "His treachery deserves a response."

Aldred swore under his breath. "What do you intend to do?"

"First, I'll seek your brother's counsel," William said.

Aldred spat on the ground. "He has no say in this."

"He knows you better than anyone here," William said, turning to his new ally. "Well, Wulfstan? What do you advise?"

Conflict flared in Wulfstan's eyes. Then it died as he regarded his brother. "Kill him."

Lightning flashed, and Aldred drew his sword. Wulfstan and Robert backed away.

Adrenaline shot through William's body. 'Twas a call to combat, and he knew it well. With grim determination, he pulled his sword from its sheath.

A deafening thunderclap split the sky as William and Aldred circled each other.

Aldred grinned. "Finally," he said, "after all these years. Hattin had his turn. Now I have mine."

He slashed at William's face. William wrenched away, and the wind from Aldred's blade brushed his cheek. A series of thrusts followed. William blocked every one.

Aldred sneered. "Your skill with a sword is impressive," he said. "'What a pity you've none with the ladies."

Hate forged a fever in William's blood, but he fought its seductive song. An angry swordsman was a dead one.

"What?" Aldred taunted. "No response? I have it on good authority your lovemaking is tame."

A muscle twitched in William's jaw, but he made no reply.

"Sahar regaled me with tales of your boring performance," Aldred persisted. "No wonder your wife drank the poison. She'd rather die than lie beneath you."

William pitched forward. He tackled Aldred to the ground, knocking the sword from Aldred's hand. They grappled in the dust to the sound of men's shouts and crackling thunder.

Aldred reached for his sword. William punched him in the nose. Stunned only for an instant, Aldred grabbed his sword and clipped William's temple with the pommel.

Pain shot through William's head. He fell backward but rolled aside as Aldred's sword smote the ground where he'd lain. He scrambled to his feet, sword in hand.

Aldred stabbed William's arm, exactly where the poisoned arrow had struck. Wincing, William tightened his grip on his sword.

Aldred laughed, despite the blood trickling from his nose. "A reminder, Norman."

"Believe me," William said through his teeth, "I need none."

The clash of steel resumed. Aldred jabbed and lunged. William blocked and parried.

A strange sense of calm enveloped William as he deflected attack after attack. At last, their cross-guards locked. Their faces were mere inches apart. William could smell Aldred's fetid breath. And he knew what he must do.

"You're finished, Aldred," he said.

The Saxon's eyes were wide, crazy. "Why? Because you're handy with a sword? Because my brother betrayed me?"

William smiled. "Because you're a fool."

Aldred snarled and broke away from him. With both hands, he raised his sword above his head. He was off-balance, vulnerable.

William thrust his blade into Aldred's chest.

A woman screamed. The crowd hushed.

Aldred froze, his arms above his head, his eyes open wide. The sword fell from his hands and plunked on the bailey floor. He dropped beside it, face-down in the dust.

A gurgle rose from his throat. As the rain began to fall, he stilled.

Aldred the Merciless was dead.

Chapter Twenty-Four

Rain thrashed the keep. Inside, a growing chill sharpened the air. Yet William refused the solace of a fire and paced in front of the solar's barren hearth. He'd allowed Tilda to treat his wounds but had rejected her offer of food. It seemed profane to consider his own comfort while above, Emma fought for her life.

He'd spared only a glance for Aldred's lifeless body before racing to Emma's side, but Meg immediately sent him away. Once again, he was forced to wait. Alone. And the drone of voices in the great hall waxed on.

One by one, Ravenwood's people trickled into the hall. The instant they learned of Emma's condition, they came. They seemed to need each other.

William stopped pacing and stared at the planked floor. He didn't want to need anyone. He'd devoted his life to that end, ever since his ordeal in the Holy Land.

In sooth, even before then, he thought.

He looked up as Robert and John, the steward, entered the solar.

"Come, William," said Robert. "You've been brooding long enough."

William sighed. "'Tis not every day one kills a man, though you'd think I'd be used to it by now."

"You had to do it," Robert said.

John nodded. "We all approve," he said. "Aldred

deserved it, and his death is good news for Nihtscua."

Robert fingered the dagger at his waist. "But that's not why we're here."

John stepped forward. "My lord, the people need you. They fear so for Lady Ravenwood."

William rubbed his eyes. "I've no comfort to give. Not now."

"You have," Robert argued, "because you share their suffering."

"Let the people see you," John pleaded. "Be with them."

William looked from one man to the other. He listened to the voices invading the solar. Above the din, a child sobbed.

He swallowed hard. "I'll go."

Hand on heart, John sighed. Robert nodded his approval. Then together, the three men left the solar.

The moment William stepped foot in the hall, the magnitude of Ravenwood's distress hit him. The room was packed, just as it had been on his wedding day, and all eyes looked to him. He waded through a sea of anxious faces to the dais, but he didn't climb onto it. He stood before it, on the same level as everyone else, and turned around.

An elderly woman hobbled forward. "My lord," she said, "'tis good you've come. I want you to know, I'm praying for her ladyship. She visited me every day when I was ill. If angels walk the earth, she must be one of them."

She stepped back, and a gangly stable boy took her place.

"My lord," he said, "Lady Ravenwood must get well. She mended my puppy's leg, and now he can run."

The huntsman came up alongside the stable boy. "Her ladyship heals the hounds," he said. Then his gaze dropped to the floor. "They know her voice like they know mine."

An elderly man with hunched shoulders and faded blue eyes stood beside the huntsman. "My lord," he said, clasping his hands together, "I'm Roderic, the beekeeper. My assistant would be lost without her ladyship's help. As I would be, without her kindness."

One after another, the people spoke. Each story, each compassionate word, hammered William like the torrential rain pounding the keep. He absorbed it all, adding their memories to his, until his throat ached.

Suddenly, he felt a tug at his tunic. He looked down and stared into a pair of innocent, brown eyes, brimming with tears. They belonged to Martin, Tilda's five-year-old brother. William thought of the boy's imaginary bout with Saracens...and how tightly his small arms had hugged Emma.

"Please," Martin said, his lips quivering. "Don't let Lady Ravenwood die."

William's heart lurched. Gently, he placed his hand on Martin's tousled, red hair. "I'll do what I can."

The weight of Ravenwood's sorrow pressed down on him, and his emotions threatened to overflow. Brusquely, he turned and strode from the hall. He climbed the steps two at a time to his bedchamber.

As he pushed open the door, three tired faces turned to him. Meg, Wulfstan, and Father Cedric stood beside the bed, blocking his view of Emma. All he could see was the slight mound in the fur coverlets, beneath which lay Emma's feet.

He stepped over the threshold, and the warmth from the hearth reached out to him. "I must see my wife," he said. "How does she fare?"

Meg's expression was grim. "Not as well as I'd like."

His chest tightened. His throat burned.

Wulfstan turned to Meg and placed his hands on her shoulders. "We've done all we can," he said. "The rest is up to her."

Meg nodded in silence.

"I'll be below if you need me," Wulfstan said, dropping his arms. He gave William a sympathetic glance, then left the chamber.

William found his voice. "Father Cedric," he said, "the people have gathered in the hall. They could use your support."

"I shall go to them," the priest replied, closing his prayer book. "Keep faith, Meg...my lord."

Father Cedric stepped away from the bed. At last, William glimpsed Emma's face. 'Twas flushed, devoid of expression.

He rushed forward. Meg patted his arm in a motherly manner.

"You sit with Emma," she said as the door thudded closed. "I'll rest by the fire."

Her hoarse voice tugged at his memory. "Does your head pain you?" he asked.

"Not overmuch," she said. "Save your concern, and your prayers, for Emma."

He nodded. As Meg shuffled toward the fire, he focused again on his wife.

He touched her fevered brow, then took her hand in his. Her flesh was unthinkably hot. Her hand was so small.

The questions he'd buried all day pushed their way to the surface. What if she never opened her eyes? Never smiled, never laughed, never talked with him again?

His soul knew the answer. If she died, he would go on. But a part of him would be lost forever.

He wanted to shake her, to will her awake. Instead, he squeezed her hand and sent her a message, soul to soul.

Live, Emma, he pleaded. *Live.*

****

A long time later, Meg asked William to leave. Reluctantly, he returned to the solar, where a fire now brightened the hearth. Robert and Wulfstan sat before it, sipping from pewter cups. The small table between them held a large pitcher and a platter of sliced meats and bread.

William's stomach rumbled, but he ignored it. Physically and emotionally drained, he claimed the seat beside Robert and stared into the flames.

"Would you like some wine?" Robert asked.

"No," said William.

"Some food, perhaps?" Wulfstan offered.

"Not now."

Robert sighed heavily. "When did you last eat?"

"Supper last night." *With Emma.*

Wulfstan leaned forward. "Think of all that has happened since then."

William turned to him. "Aye. I killed your brother."

"I know," said Wulfstan. "I was there."

William's eyes narrowed. "You don't mourn his

loss?"

Wulfstan shook his head. "Aldred lived to hurt others. Who knows what darker ends he would've sought next?"

"I misjudged you," William said. "For that, I'm sorry."

Wulfstan's blue eyes widened.

"Do my ears deceive me?" Robert asked.

"They do not," William said, his gaze still on Wulfstan. "And I want to you to know, I appreciate your efforts to help Lady Ravenwood."

Wulfstan blinked. "Are you saying—"

"Aye," said William. "Thank you."

Chapter Twenty-Five

Emma thought she heard her mother calling to her. But how? From within the womb before birth? From the mysterious realm of spirit? The harmonious sound beckoned, beseeched her to wake.

She opened her eyes. Two shadows loomed over her, but slowly, her vision focused.

"Meg," she murmured.

The elderly woman smiled. "Child, you're awake."

"Barely," Emma said, fighting the urge to sleep. She shifted her gaze. "William."

"Emma," he said. Relief resonated in his deep, beloved voice.

Meg lifted Emma's head a few inches and pressed a cup to her lips. "Here, drink some wine."

Emma swallowed several sips. She'd never been so thirsty in her life.

"Not too much now," Meg said. She withdrew the cup and let Emma's head rest again on the pillow. "You've been racked with fever for two days, ever since..."

The memory of betrayal came flooding back. "I remember," Emma said. "Where is Gertrude?"

"We don't know," said William. "She supposedly fled to Nihtscua, but no one there has seen her."

"And Aldred?"

"Dead."

She closed her eyes. "God be praised."

"Not to mention your husband," Meg said.

Emma looked up at him. "Did you—"

"Aye. I killed him."

"And you're safe," she said with a smile.

His warm hand smoothed her brow. "I am," he said. "And so are you."

"Thanks to Wulfstan," said Meg.

William cocked an eyebrow at the older woman. "You had something to do with it."

Meg grinned. "Something."

Emma sighed. "I'm too trusting."

"No one blames you for trusting Gertrude," William said.

Her stomach quivered. "Don't be angry, William."

"I'm not," he said.

"You will be once you've heard what I have to say. Promise me you'll try to understand."

He furrowed his brow, but nodded. "I promise."

"The morning Wulfstan arrived, I had a revelation. I suddenly knew, without a doubt, that I loved you and wanted to give myself to you fully."

With a tender half-smile, he regarded her. "Do you mean what I think you do?"

"If you think I want you in my bed, then you're right."

His eyes held a glint of mischief. Then he sobered. "Why would I be angry about that?"

"Just listen," she said. "I hoped that if we shared the act of love, I'd eventually earn yours. But until I did, I needed protection from the curse. So I thought of a temporary solution."

"What solution?"

She took a deep breath. "The drink, or what I thought I was drinking, was supposed to prevent pregnancy. But only until you loved me."

A shadow fell over his face.

Meg placed a hand on his arm. "She was still taking a chance. Such medicine is unreliable."

Emma's heart swelled. "'Twas worth the risk. Believe me, William, I never meant to hurt you, and I want to give you heirs. But I also want to live."

His gaze seemed riveted on a ray of sunlight that streamed through the open window to the foot of the bed. But finally, he met her gaze.

"I think I understand," he said.

The warmth in his dark eyes infused her with hope. "Thank you," she said.

He gave her a look full of meaning. "You are my wife. Your pain is mine."

She smiled, recalling the night she'd uttered similar words to him. Obviously, they'd made their mark.

"Shall I leave you two alone?" Meg asked.

He shook his head. "I must away. Robert and I are off to Nihtscua to look for Gertrude. Wulfstan has agreed to help us."

Emma yawned. Her eyelids felt heavy. "How long will you be gone?" she asked.

"A fortnight at most."

"So long?"

With a grin, he caressed her cheek. "We've a lot of ground to cover, including the North Woods. But I'll return as soon as possible. In the meantime, you must rest and regain your strength. Do as Meg tells you."

"Listen to the man, Emma," Meg said spiritedly.

Emma's eyes closed of their own accord. She could

listen to no one and nothing but the siren song of sleep.

****

Ten days later, Emma was fully recovered. She spent the crisp, autumn morning flitting between the herb garden and her workshop. In the afternoon, she chatted with servants picking fruit in the orchards.

After an ample, delicious supper, she retired to the solar to enjoy the crackling fire and indulge in the activity which made her feel closest to William. With a steady hand, she pressed her quill to the parchment and practiced writing Arabic characters.

She longed for his return. Ten days without him had seemed a lifetime.

With a sigh, she bent over the long, candle-crowded table and wrote a full word. To her right was Meg; to her left, Tilda. Both women leaned forward to examine Emma's work.

"What is it?" Tilda asked.

"My name," Emma answered.

"It looks a bit odd," Tilda said.

"Perhaps," said Meg. "But things that are odd are often the most beautiful."

Emma smiled. "'Tis exotic."

Suddenly, a cacophony of male voices and horse hooves sounded in the bailey. Emma's heart did a somersault. She looked to Tilda, then Meg. "Do you think..." she began, but the words tripped on her tongue.

Meg grinned. "That Lord Ravenwood is back?"

Emma couldn't speak. She nodded.

Meg tilted her head. "There's only one way to know."

Emma dropped the quill. She grasped the skirt of

her red tunic, lifting it six inches off the floor. Ladies weren't supposed to grab their skirts, but at that moment, she didn't care. She dashed from the solar to the forebuilding, then halted at the top of the stairs.

The night wind kissed her cheeks as she scanned the bailey. A host of men milled about, but only one commanded her gaze.

Clothed in his customary black, William stood beside his warhorse. Geoffrey took Thunder's rein, and William turned slowly, as though sensing Emma's stare.

"William!" she cried, waving.

He beamed up at her. Her heart leapt, and she floated down the steps. He snapped into action and crossed the courtyard with long, impatient strides.

They met at the base of the stairs. She threw herself against him and wrapped her arms around his neck.

"Raven," he murmured.

She relished the feel of his strong arms enfolding her. The rich timbre of his voice was like music, like coming home.

"I missed you," she said against his chest.

"And I you."

Warmed by his admission, she lifted her head and gazed into his luminous, black eyes. "You must be hungry and longing for the fire," she said. "Shall we go inside?"

"Kiss me first."

She giggled. "If you insist."

His lips claimed hers, and she surrendered to a deep, soulful kiss. A full minute later, he pulled away and whispered in her ear. "I may not need a fire after all."

His hot breath tickled her ear. "I see what you mean," she said. "Perhaps a cold bath?"

He chuckled. "Come, let's go inside."

Hand in hand, they started up the stairs.

"You look well," he remarked. "Radiant, in fact."

"I followed your advice, and Meg's, of course. But tell me, where's your brother?"

"He stayed behind at Nihtscua, but he'll be back within the week. He and Wulfstan are becoming friends."

"Really? And you approve?"

"I do, though I can hardly believe it."

"Nor can I, but I'm pleased."

"I'm pleased for Nihtscua. The people will finally have a decent master, but there's much to be done. Aldred left the place in horrible repair."

"Did you find Gertrude?"

William squeezed her hand as they entered the keep. "Not a trace of her. She's simply disappeared."

"Well, as long as she stays away from Ravenwood, I'm content."

"I'd rather avenge you."

"Don't worry. I've a feeling her deeds will catch up with her, in one way or another."

As they entered the solar, Meg and Tilda looked up from the parchment on the table.

"My lord," Tilda said, bobbing a curtsy.

Meg glanced at their linked hands, then flashed William a smile. "Welcome home."

"Thank you," he replied. Then he glimpsed the parchment. "What is that?"

Meg turned to Tilda. "We'll let Emma explain," she said, winking at the handmaiden. "Won't we?"

Tilda stared at Meg for a long moment, then seemed to understand. "Aye," she said quickly.

"Enjoy your evening," Meg said. Then she and Tilda made a beeline for the door.

Snaps and whispers rose from the fire. They were the only sounds in the room, with the possible exception of Emma's thumping heart.

Alone at last, she thought.

William guided her to the table, then grinned as he studied the parchment.

"Arabic," he said. "You've been practicing."

"I have. 'Twas the next best thing to having you beside me."

He smiled. "Well, I'm beside you now," he said. Then he sobered. "And I must speak with you."

She studied his face. "About?" she prompted.

He cleared his throat. "First, I must correct you. You believe the people don't love you, but while you were ill, every one of them came to the hall. They prayed for you, cried for you, and sang your praises to the battlements. You've made an impression on Ravenwood that has nothing to do with your medicines or visions. It stems from your character and your heart. You sought the people's love, but 'twas yours all along."

She blinked back tears.

"'Tis time you accepted Ravenwood's devotion," he continued. "And…I ask you to accept mine."

She held her breath.

"I've fought a dreadful battle, Emma. I made you pay for the betrayal of another and the bitterness in my heart. 'Twas wrong of me, and I took you for granted. But when I thought I might lose you, I didn't care about

Ravenwood or the sons I'd never have. For the first time, I envisioned my life without you, and 'twas darker and colder than anything I've ever known. I want you, Emma. I need you. I...love you."

Tears trickled down her cheeks as she absorbed the magnitude of his words. The curse was broken. "I love you too," she whispered.

He took her face in his hands, and his thumbs wiped away her tears. "Don't cry," he murmured.

"I'm just so happy," she said.

He kissed her tenderly, sharing the tide of emotion as his mouth worshipped hers.

When at last he pulled away, she smiled. Sniffling, she glanced at the tapestry of "The Forest Dance" on the wall behind him.

"While the fever was upon me, I had the strangest dream," she said. "It involved that tapestry."

William looked over his shoulder, then turned back to her. "Tell me."

"I was here in the solar," she began, "and I saw you looking up at it. So I went to you and took your hand. As I touched you, you became transparent, like a ghost. Then we floated up and entered the tapestry."

His face paled.

"William?" she said.

"Go on," he urged.

She nodded. "Once we were in there, I asked you to stay with me by the fire, but you refused. Then the most extraordinary thing happened. You transformed into a raven and flew into the forest. Suddenly I was a raven, too, so I flew after you. I searched everywhere, but the forest was so dark. You were lost to me...until I heard your voice."

"A raven's voice?"

"No, your own."

"What did I say?"

"Just one word. 'Live.' You said it over and over, and I followed the sound until I found you. You were trapped in a mass of twisted branches, but somehow, you broke free. Then together, we flew out of the forest and into the light."

William turned and stared at the tapestry. "I had a similar dream, ages ago it seems."

Emma came alongside him. She slipped an arm around his waist, and his arm closed around her shoulders.

"Did it end the same way?" she asked.

"No," he answered, gazing down at her. "I might've stayed in that forest forever, if not for you. My dear, sweet raven. You braved the darkness and brought me back into the light."

Her throat tight with emotion, she looked up at his beloved face. Within his eyes, she saw everything she'd always wanted...and more.

"One thing puzzles me, though," he said, turning back to the tapestry. "What are those two small shadows at the edge of the forest?"

"I believe they're ravens."

"They weren't there before."

"William, I've studied this tapestry since I was a little girl. Those shadows have always been there."

"Why didn't I see them before?"

"Perhaps you weren't ready."

"And I'm ready now?"

Emma nodded. "I'm ready too."

Slowly, he turned to her. "For what?"

She grinned. "To give you the wedding night we should've had."

"Now?"

"Now."

****

They raced up the stairs. The bedchamber was blessedly empty, and Emma's headdress hit the floor the instant she crossed the threshold. Behind her, William grinned as he shut the door and slid the bolt home. There followed a mad, joyous rush to shed all clothing.

Finally free of her smock, she turned to him, and he kicked his braies aside. His naked body was magnificent; his arousal, obvious.

He spared a glance for the quiet hearth. "Are you sure you'll be warm enough?" he asked. "You've been ill, and there's no fire."

Her skin glowed, and her violet eyes flared with passion. "Damn the fire," she said, rushing toward him.

Laughing, he scooped her up in his arms. "You're right," he said as he carried her to the bed. "We need no fire. We'll create our own."

He laid her on the bed, then lay beside her. She luxuriated in the feel of the fur coverlets beneath her, in the musky scent of his skin, in the freedom to surrender at last to desire.

Their lips locked in a passionate kiss that banished the outside world to oblivion. Nothing mattered but the feel of flesh, the power of two souls uniting in love.

William caressed her breasts, hips, and bottom. He sucked hard on her nipples as she writhed beneath him. Her gasps and moans were like music. With a grin, he slid his hand between her legs.

Emma trembled as he touched the source of her excitement. Gently, repeatedly, his finger pushed against it. "Aye," she breathed, raising her hips.

Mad with desire, he positioned himself between her thighs. He pushed only the head of his shaft into her warm sheath. Then slowly, his finger caressed the swollen bud of her desire.

The tension built inside her, pushed her to the brink, and then…at the moment of her release, his full length thrust into her, breaking her maidenhead. She felt a mere instant of pain before spasms of pleasure swallowed it.

He groaned at the sensation of her tight, hot channel convulsing around his shaft. Kissing her forehead, he murmured, "I didn't want to hurt you."

"The pain was brief," she said. "Did you feel pleasure?"

He licked the salty sweat from her throat. "Aye, but not release."

She stared at him. "There's more?"

He chuckled and kissed the tip of her nose. "There is indeed. Shall I show you?"

She bit her lip. "You feel so big inside of me. Will there be pain?"

He shook his head. "Only delight."

"Then show me."

With a groan, he cupped her buttocks and started to move inside her.

"Oh," she said. "I never thought…I never knew…"

His thrusts grew harder, faster. She moaned and wrapped her legs around him, sensing an even greater pleasure just beyond her reach. She dug her fingernails into his back and bit his shoulder.

"My wild raven," he rasped. "This is our storm. Fly into it. Soar with me to heaven."

Epilogue

Ten months later

All of Ravenwood had gathered in the great hall. With hands clasped behind his back, William paced up and down the dais.

Robert stood just below him in front of the dais. "Be still, Brother," he said. "You're making me nervous."

William halted. "*You're* nervous? She's my wife. And childbirth is a dangerous business."

"True, but Meg is with her. All will be well."

"It had better be."

Suddenly, the hall went quiet. William regarded the throng of people then turned in the direction they stared.

Tilda stood in the archway. "My lord," she said with a curtsy, "Ravenwood has a son."

"And Lady Ravenwood?" he asked.

She smiled. "Her ladyship is well and waiting for you."

Relief coursed through him. The crowd cheered, and his heart swelled.

I have a son, he thought, and he could hardly believe it. 'Twas a dream come true.

Robert clapped him on the back. "Congratulations," he shouted above the clamor.

"Thank you," William yelled back. He bolted out of the hall and flew up the stairs.

Meg beamed at him as he entered the bedchamber. Then she stepped aside so he could see his family. Propped up by pillows, Emma sat up in bed. She looked tired but radiant all the same. She smiled at the small bundle in her arms, then at him.

"William," she said. "Come and meet your son."

He hurried forward and captured her lips in a brief, tender kiss. Then he peered at the tiny scrap of magic swathed in linen. "He's incredible."

"He's asleep," Emma replied.

Meg approached the bed. "And he's perfect in every way," she said.

William puffed out his chest. "Of course he is. He's my son."

"Then I trust he has your modesty," Emma teased.

"Careful," he said with a grin. "You'll wake him with your slurs."

"I wouldn't mind. I'm eager to see his eyes again."

"I'm eager to see how he rides a horse."

Emma giggled. "You'll have to wait a few years for that."

He nodded. "Perhaps you're right. Until then, he can ride on my shoulders. And when he's a bit older, my back."

Meg laughed. "So much for the dread reputation of William the Storm."

He cocked an eyebrow at her. "Oh, I don't know. He still exists."

Emma's violet eyes shimmered. "But now he's my storm," she said with a smile.

William's heart was full, complete. He lifted

Emma's hand and kissed it with all of the joy that sang inside him. "And so shall I be," he said, "forever."

A word about the author...

Judith Sterling is a pseudonym for Judith Marshall, whose nonfiction books *My Conversations with Angels* and *Past Lives, Present Stories* have been translated into multiple languages. She has an MA in linguistics and a BA in history, with a minor in British Studies. Born in that sauna called Florida, she craved cooler climes, and once the travel bug bit, she lived in England, Scotland, Sweden, Wisconsin, Virginia, and on the island of Nantucket. She currently lives in Salem, Massachusetts, with her husband and their identical twin sons.

http://judithmarshallauthor.com

Made in the USA
Lexington, KY
15 October 2016